Also by Mia Couto

Confession
of the Lioness

Confession
of the Lioness

Mia Couto

TRANSLATED FROM THE PORTUGUESE
BY DAVID BROOKSHAW

FARRAR, STRAUS AND GIROUX ◆ NEW YORK

Farrar, Straus and Giroux
18 West 18th Street, New York 10011

Copyright © 2012 by Editorial Caminho
Translation copyright © 2015 by David Brookshaw
All rights reserved
Printed in the United States of America
Originally published in 2012 by Editorial Caminho, Portugal, as *A Confissão da Leoa*
English translation published in the United States by Farrar, Straus and Giroux
First American edition, 2015

Library of Congress Cataloging-in-Publication Data
Couto, Mia, 1955–
    [Confissão da leoa. English]
    Confession of the lioness / Mia Couto ; translated from the Portuguese / by
David Brookshaw. — First American edition.
        pages   cm
    ISBN 978-0-374-12923-1 (hardcover) — ISBN 978-0-374-71095-8 (e-book)
    I. Brookshaw, David, translator.   II. Title.

PQ9939.C68 C6613 2015
869.3'42—dc23

                                                                  2014039381

Designed by Abby Kagan

Farrar, Straus and Giroux books may be purchased for educational, business, or
promotional use. For information on bulk purchases, please contact the Macmillan
Corporate and Premium Sales Department at 1-800-221-7945, extension 5442, or
write to specialmarkets@macmillan.com.

www.fsgbooks.com
www.twitter.com/fsgbooks • www.facebook.com/fsgbooks

1   3   5   7   9   10   8   6   4   2

Until lions invent their own stories, hunters will always be the heroes of their hunting narratives.

—AFRICAN PROVERB

Contents

Author's Note

In 2008, the company I work for sent fifteen young people to serve as environmental field officers during a program of seismic prospecting in Cabo Delgado, northern Mozambique. During the same period and in the same region, lions began to attack people. Within a few weeks, there were more than ten fatal attacks. This number increased to twenty in about four months.

Our young colleagues were working in the bush, sleeping in campaign tents, and moving around on foot between villages. They were an easy target for the lions. Hunters were urgently needed in order to provide protection. And, of course, this urgency was all the greater because of the need to protect the country folk of the area. Our advice to the oil company was that it should take complete responsibility for protecting against this threat: The lions that had been eating people needed to be eliminated. Two experienced hunters were contracted and traveled from Maputo to Palma, the town at the center of these attacks. Once in town, they recruited other, local hunters to join the operation. In the meantime, the number of victims killed had increased to twenty-six.

The hunters underwent two months of frustration and terror, responding to daily calls for help until they managed to kill the murderous lions. But it wasn't just these difficulties they had to face. It was suggested to them time after time that the real culprits were inhabitants of the invisible world, where rifles and bullets were no use at all. Gradually, the hunters realized that the mysteries they were having to confront were merely symptoms of social conflicts for which they had no adequate solution.

I lived through this whole situation at close quarters. The frequent visits I made to where this drama was taking place gave me the idea for the story that I am about to tell, which was inspired by real facts and people.

Confession
of the Lioness

- Mary
- Water

Mariamar's Version

ONE

The News

Blessed is the lion that the man will eat, for the lion will become human; and cursed is the man the lion will eat, for the lion will become human.

—GOSPEL ACCORDING TO THOMAS

God was once a woman. Before he exiled himself far from his creation, and while he had still not assumed the name of Nungu, the current Lord of the Universe looked like all the mothers in this world. In this other time, we spoke the same language as the oceans, the land, and the heavens. According to my grandfather, that kingdom perished long ago. But somewhere within us, there remains the memory of that far-off age. Illusions and certainties survive that have been passed on from one generation to another in our village of Kulumani. We all know, for example, that the sky is as yet unfinished. It's the women who, for millennia, have been weaving its infinite veil. When their bellies grow round, a piece of sky is added. Conversely, when they lose a child, this piece of firmament withers away.

Maybe this is why my mother, Hanifa Assulua, kept watching the clouds during the burial of her eldest daughter. My sister Silência was the most recent victim of the lions, which have been tormenting our village for some weeks now.

As she died disfigured, they laid what remained of her body on its left-hand side, with the head turned to the east and the feet turned to the south. During the ceremony, my mother seemed to be dancing: Time and again she would bend over a pitcher which she had made with her own hands. She sprinkled the surrounding earth with water and then stamped both her feet to the same rhythm as someone sowing seeds.

As she returned from the funeral, there was too much sky in my poor mother's eyes. It was only a short walk home: The family graveyard was on the outskirts of the village. Hanifa made a brief detour along the River Lideia to complete her ritual cleansing by bathing in its waters, while farther back, I erased the footprints leading to the grave.

Shake your feet, dust likes to travel.

In the hallowed ground of our graveyard stood yet another cross, showing that we were different from the Muslims and from the pagans. I know now: If we place a tombstone over the dead, it's not out of respect. It's out of fear. We're afraid they'll come back. Over time, this fear becomes greater than our yearning for them.

All the members of the family respected the order: The route back was altogether different from that taken to go. Nevertheless, my mind could not rid itself of the persistent image: Silência's body being carried on shoulders, wrapped in white sheets that swayed like broken wings.

When we reached our front door, my mother looked at the house as if she were blaming it: so alive, so ancient, so timeless. Our house was different from the other huts. It was made of cement, had a tin roof, and was equipped with bedrooms, a living room, and an inside kitchen. There were rugs strewn on the floor and dusty curtains hung in the windows. We were also different from the other inhabitants of Kulumani. In particular my mother, Hanifa Assulua, was different, for she had some education, and was the daughter of educated parents. On our way back from the funeral, I noticed how beautiful she was: Even with her head shaved in compliance with her mourning, her countenance belied her grief. For some time, she eyed me as if weighing up how precious I was to her. I thought there was a maternal tenderness in her look. But her words were shaped by other feelings:

You'll never have to experience a mother's grief.

Please, Mother, I've just lost my sister, I said.

You'll never lose a daughter. It was God who wished it thus.

And she turned her back. Having taken off her shoes, she crossed the threshold and took to her bed. One can bury a daughter, that's true. She had already done so before. But one never stops saying farewell. No one needs a mother's attention more than a dead child.

At this point, my father asked the mourning women to leave our yard. He entered the darkened house and, leaning over his wife, asked:

Why did you shave your head? Are we not Christians?

Hanifa shrugged. At that particular moment, she was nothing at all. The wailing of the women mourners had ceased and she couldn't stand the vast silence.

So what shall we do now, ntwangu?

Like all women in Kulumani, she called her husband *ntwangu.* The man's name was Genito Serafim Mpepe. But out of respect, she never addressed him by his name. Yes, we were educated, but we were too much a part of Kulumani. All our present was made up of our past. At that moment, her husband nestled up to her and spoke with a gentleness that she wasn't used to, each word a cloud patching up the skies.

What shall we do now? Well, now . . . now we shall live, woman.

I don't know how to live anymore, ntwangu.

No one knows how to. But that is what our daughter is asking us to do: to live.

Don't talk to me about what our daughter asked. You never listened to her.

Not now! Don't talk about that now, woman.

You didn't understand my question: What shall we do with that bit of our daughter we didn't bury?

I don't want to talk about that. Let's sleep.

She raised herself, leaning on her elbow. Her eyes were dilated, like those of someone who had drowned.

But our Silência . . .

Quiet, woman! Have you forgotten that we can never again utter our daughter's name?

I need to know: Which bits of her body couldn't we bury?

I've already told you to be quiet, woman.

His voice trembled, leaflike: My father was struggling with inner demons. The blood-soaked sack containing his daughter's remains still dripped in his memory. And once again he was assailed by a recollection that could never be laid to rest: the sudden confusion of voices and panic that had woken him in the early hours of the previous day. Genito Mpepe had crossed the yard expecting tragedy. Moments before, he had heard the lions prowling around the house. Suddenly there were roars, cries, wails dispersing in the air, the world sank out of sight in shattered pieces: Nothing remained within him. To forget such an event, it would be necessary never to have lived.

The heart? Hanifa persisted.

Again? Didn't I tell you to keep quiet?

Did we bury her heart? You know very well what they do with the heart...

My father took a deep breath, and contemplated the old clothes hanging from the rafters. He didn't feel any different from those garments, drooping shapelessly and without soul in the emptiness. His voice returned to him, and he spoke softly once again:

Think of it this way, woman: A child doesn't have a grave.

I don't want to listen to this, I'm going out.

Going out?

I'm going to get what's left of our daughter out there in the bush.

You're not going. You're not leaving the house.

No one's going to stop me.

She would leave home, she would go beyond the paths created by people, her feet would bleed, her eyes would burn from their encounter with the sun, but she would go and get what remained of Silência, forever her little girl-child. Blocking her way, her husband threatened:

I'm going to tie you with a rope, like an animal.

Tie me up, then. I've been no more than an animal for a long time. You've been sleeping with an animal in your bed for a long time now...

That put an end to the discussion. Hanifa silently curled up, her arms snuggled between her legs, as if she wanted to give in to sleep.

Are you going to sleep on the floor? Genito asked.

She lay on the ground, her head resting on the stony floor. She wanted to listen to the world's insides. The women of Kulumani know secrets. They know, for example, that within their mother's womb, babies, at a given moment, change position. Throughout the world, they turn on themselves, obeying a single voice from deep within the earth. The same happens with the dead: On the same night—and it can only happen on that particular night—they are all ordered to turn over in the earth's belly. This is when lights glow over their graves, a swirling of silvery dust. Whoever sleeps with his (or her) ear to the ground hears this gyration of the dead. It was for this reason, unknown to Genito, that Hanifa refused a bed and a pillow. Flat out on the floor, she was listening to the earth. It wouldn't be long before her daughter made herself felt. Who knows, maybe the twins, Uminha and Igualita, the ones who had died before, would deliver her messages from the other side of the world.

Her husband didn't go to bed: He knew that he was in for a long night. The memory of his daughter's mangled body would keep sleep at bay. The lion's roar would echo within him, lacerating his sleepless hours. He remained for a while on the veranda, peering into the darkness. Maybe the stillness would bring him respite. But silence is an egg in reverse: The shell is someone else's, but it's we who get broken.

One doubt consumed him: How had the tragedy occurred? Had his daughter left the house in the middle of the night? And if that had been the case, was it her intention to end her life? Or, conversely, had the lion broken into the house, more burglar than beast?

Suddenly the whole world was shattered: The peace of the bush was interrupted by the sound of furtive steps. Genito's heart thumped hard against his chest. What was happening was what always happened: The lions were coming back to eat what they'd left behind the previous day.

Then, unexpectedly, like a man possessed, he started yelling, while running this way and that:

I know you're there, creatures of the devil! Show yourselves, I want to see you come out of the bush, you're vantumi va vanu!

I watched him in this frenzied state from the window, as he challenged the lion-people, the *vantumi va vanu*. All of a sudden he flopped to the ground as if his knees had been smashed. He raised his head slowly and saw that he was in the embrace of a bat's dark wings. He couldn't hear a sound, not even the rustling of a wing or a leaf above his head. Genito Mpepe was a tracker—he knew all the invisible signs of the savanna. He had often told me: Only humans recognize silence. For all the other creatures, the world is never silent and even the grass growing and the petals opening make a huge noise. In the bush, the animals live by listening. That's what my father envied at that moment: He wished he were an animal. And far from human beings, to be able to return to his lair and fall asleep without pity or guilt.

I know you're there!

This time his words were no longer laden with rage. Hoarseness caused his voice to weaken. Repeating his curses, he returned to the house to seek refuge in his bedroom. His wife was still lying curled up on the floor, just as he had left her. As he was covering her with a blanket, Hanifa Assulua woke with a start, and, clinging furiously to her husband's body, she exclaimed:

Let's make love!

Now?

Yes. Now!

You're out of your mind, Hanifa. You don't know what you're saying.

Are you refusing me, husband? Don't you want a quick one?

You know that we can't. We're in mourning—the whole village will be sullied.

That's what I want: the village, the whole world, to be sullied.

Hanifa, listen to me: Time will pass, folk will forget. People even forget they're alive.

I haven't been alive for a long time. Now I've stopped being a person.

My father looked at her as if she were a stranger. His wife had never spoken like that before. In fact, she almost never spoke. She had always been contained, kept in the shadows. After the twins had died, she never again uttered a word. So much so that her husband would occasionally ask:

Are you alive, Hanifa Assulua?

But it wasn't that she spoke so little. For her, life had become a foreign language. Once again, his wife was preparing herself for this absence, Genito thought, without noticing that Hanifa, in the darkness, was taking off her clothes. Once naked, she hugged him from behind and Genito Mpepe succumbed to her serpent's embrace. He seemed to have surrendered, when he suddenly shook his wife and beat a hurried retreat to the yard. Then he disappeared into the darkness.

In the hidden recess of her room, my mother gave herself over to brazen caresses, as if her man were really with her. And so, in this way, she was in command, galloping on her own croup, dancing over her own fire. She sweated and groaned:

Don't stop, Genito! Don't stop!

That's when she became aware of the smell of sweat. A sour, intense smell like that of wild animals. Afterward, she heard the grunt. Then it occurred to my mother that it wasn't her man who was on top of her, but a creature from the bush, thirsty for her blood. During the act of love, Genito Mpepe had turned into a wild beast that was devouring her. Weakened by his fervor, she was helpless, at the mercy of his feline appetite.

I'm mad, she thought, while she closed her eyes and took a deep breath. But when she felt the claw tear her neck, Hanifa screamed so loudly that, for a moment, she didn't know whether it was out of pain or pleasure. My father came to help her, unaware of what was happening. His wife crossed the threshold in the opposite direction and Genito was unable to stop her, in her frenzied haste, from bursting out into the yard.

If she had been mistress of her will, our mother would have escaped in endless flight. But Kulumani was a closed place, surrounded by geography and atrophied by fear. Hanifa Assulua came to a halt at the entrance to the yard, next to the hedge of thorns that protected us from the bush. Raising her hands to her head, she brought them down over her face as if she were wiping away a cobweb:

I've destroyed this place! I've destroyed Kulumani!

This is what the village would say: that Genito Serafim Mpepe's wife hadn't waited for the ground to grow cold. Sex on a day of mourning, when the village was still fired up: There was no worse contamination. By making love on that day—and even worse by making love to herself—Hanifa Assulua had offended all our ancestors.

Returning to her resting place, my poor mother bore the burden of night, floating between slumber and wakefulness. When early morning came, she heard Genito Mpepe's sleepy steps.

Are you getting up early, husband?

Every morning, our mother would be up before sunrise: She'd collect firewood, light the stove, prepare food, work the allotment, dig over the earth—all this she did by herself. Now, for no apparent reason, was her husband sharing the burden of her reality?

I have some news, Genito Mpepe announced solemnly.

News? You know, ntwangu: *In Kulumani, the only news we get is when an owl hoots.*

People are coming. People from outside.

People? Real people?

They're coming from the capital.

My mother remained silent, coming to terms with her astonishment. Her husband was making it up. No news or strangers had turned up there for centuries...

How long have you known this piece of news?

Some days.

You know it's a sin.

What?

It's dangerous to know what's going on, it's a sin to spread news. Do you think God will forgive us?

Without waiting for an answer, Hanifa waved her arms about, as if she were warding off ghosts, entangling herself in the foliage that framed her. She raised her hand to her shoulder, and felt the flow of blood.

What's this, ntwangu? *Who scratched me?*

No one. The thorns, it was the acacia thorns. I've got to cut that tree back.

It wasn't the tree. Someone scratched me. Look at my shoulder: There are fingernail marks, someone clawed me.

And they argued. But both were right. In the village, even the plants have claws. In Kulumani, all living things are trained to bite. Birds devour the sky, branches rip the clouds, rain bites the earth, the dead use their teeth to reap revenge on their fate.

Hanifa gazed at the forest aghast. Her face wore the expression of an alarmed gazelle.

There's someone out there in the dark, ntwangu.

Calm down, woman.

There's someone listening to us. Let's go back inside.

The first light of day was beginning to dawn: It wouldn't be long before one could move around the house without the help of a lamp. On top of the cupboard, the oil lamp was still flickering. Suddenly Hanifa once again had that pleasant feeling that the kitchen had its own moon. As she hadn't been favored by the sun, at least she could enjoy a moonlit ceiling. She gained confidence and thought about challenging her husband, declaring in a loud voice:

I don't want any of your relatives here today. They'll be rushing over here with their commiseration. Tomorrow, when I'm a widow, they'll be in an even greater hurry to steal everything from me.

But she said nothing. She already considered herself a widow. All that was needed was for Genito Mpepe to accept his own absence.

Husband, are the ones who are coming real people?

Yes, they are.

Are you sure?

Certified authentic people, people born and bred. Among them, there's a hunter.

The bucket she was carrying in her left hand fell to the ground, and water flowed all over the yard. The broom in Hanifa's hand now became a sword to fight off demons.

A hunter? she asked in a whisper.

It's him, it's the one you're thinking of: the mulatto hunter.

At first the woman stood there motionless. Then, suddenly, decisiveness seized her: She slipped into her sandals, covered her head with a scarf, and declared that she was leaving.

Where are you going, woman?

I don't know, but I'm going to do what you never did. I'm going out onto the road, I'm going to ambush him, I'm going to kill that hunter. That man mustn't get to Kulumani.

Don't be crazy, woman. We need him, we need him to kill these damned lions.

Don't you understand, ntwangu? *That man is going to take Mariamar away from me, he's going to take my last daughter away to the city.*

Would you prefer Mariamar to be killed by lions?

His wife didn't answer. "Prefer" was not a verb that had been made for her. How can someone who has never learned to love have preferences?

If you don't let me leave now, husband, I promise I'll run away.

The man seized her by the wrists and pushed her up against the old cupboard, knocking over the lamp. Hanifa saw her little moon dissolving into blue flames across the kitchen floor.

I need to stop that mulatto. She sighed, vanquished.

At this point, I decided to intervene to defend my mother. When he saw me emerge from the shadows, my father's fury was rekindled: He raised his arm, ready to impose his kingdom's rule.

Are you going to hit me, Father?

He stared at me, perplexed: Whenever anger gets the better of me, my eyes flash intensely. Genito Mpepe looked down, unable to face me.

Do you know who summoned the hunter? I asked.

Everyone knows: It was the people from the project, the ones from the company, my father replied.

That's a lie. It was the lions that summoned the hunter. And do you know who summoned the lions?

I'm not going to answer.

It was me. I'm the one who summoned the lions.

I'm going to tell you something, so listen carefully, my father declared angrily. *Don't look at me while I'm talking. Or have you lost all respect?*

I looked down, just as the women of Kulumani do. And I became a daughter again while Genito regained the authority that had escaped him for some moments.

I want you to shut yourself away here when this hunter arrives. Do you hear?

Yes.

While these people are in Kulumani, you're not to stick so much as your nose outside.

Silence descended on the room once more. My mother and I sat down on the floor as if it were the only place left in the world. I patted her shoulder in an attempt to show comfort. She avoided me. In an instant, the order of the universe had been reestablished: we women on the ground; our father pacing up and down, in and out of the kitchen, displaying his mastery of the house. Once more, we were governed by those laws that neither God teaches nor Man explains. Suddenly Genito Mpepe stopped in the middle of the house and, opening his arms, declared:

I know what the solution is: We let the mulatto come, we leave him to kill the lions. But then we won't allow him to leave.

Are you going to kill him? I asked, alarmed.

Am I the sort of person who kills people? The one who's going to kill him is you.

Me?

It's the lions you summoned who are going to kill him.

The Hunter's Diary

ONE

The Advertisement

There's only one way to escape from a place: It's by abandoning ourselves. There's only one way to abandon ourselves: It's by loving someone.

—EXCERPT PILFERED FROM THE WRITER'S NOTEBOOKS

It's two in the morning and I can't sleep. A few hours from now, they'll announce the result of the contest. That's when I'll know whether I've been selected to go and hunt the lions in Kulumani. I never thought I'd rejoice so much at being chosen. I'm in dire need of sleep. That's because I want to get away from myself. I want to sleep so as not to exist.

———

The sun's nearly up and I'm still wrestling with the sheets. My only ailment is this: insomnia broken by brief snatches of sleep from which I wake with a start. When it comes down to it, I sleep like the animals I hunt for a living: the jumpy wakefulness of one who knows that too much inattention can be fatal.

To summon sleep, I resort to the ploy my mother used when it was our bedtime. I remember her favorite story, a legend from her native region. This is how she would tell it:

In the old days, there was nothing but night. And God shepherded the stars in the sky. When he gave them more food, they would grow fat and their bellies would burst with light. At that time, all the stars ate, and all glowed with the same joy. The days were not yet born, and that was why Time advanced on only one leg. And everything was so slow up there in the endless firmament! Until, among the shepherd's flock, a star was born that aspired to be bigger than all the others. This star was called Sun, and it soon took over the celestial pastures, banishing the other stars afar, so that they began to fade. For the first time, there were stars that suffered and became so pale that they were swallowed up by the darkness. The Sun flaunted its grandeur more and more, lordly over its domains and proud of its name, so redolent of masculinity. And so he gave himself the title of lord of all the stars and planets, assuming all the arrogance of the center of the Universe. It wasn't long before he declared that it was he who had created God. But in fact what had happened was that with the Sun now so vast and sovereign, Day had been born. Night only dared to approach when the Sun, tired at last, decided to go to bed. With the advent of Day, men forgot the endless time when all stars shone with the same degree of happiness. And they forgot the lesson of the Night, who had always been a queen without ever having to rule.

This was the story. Forty years on and this maternal comfort has no effect. It won't be long before I know whether I'm going back to the bush, where men have forgotten all the lessons learned. It'll be my last hunting expedition. And once again, the first voice I ever heard echoes in my mind: *And everything was so slow up there in the endless firmament.*

First thing in the morning, having scarcely slept, I get ready to go to the offices of the newspaper, two blocks down from where I live. But before I leave, I take my old rifle out of the cupboard. I lay it across my legs and caress it with the loving care of a violinist. My name is engraved in the breech: *Archangel Bullseye—hunter.* My old father must be proud of the way an old family tradition has lived on through me. It was this tradition that justified our name: We Bullseyes always hit the target.

I'm a hunter—I know what it is to pursue prey. Yet all my life, I've been the one pursued. I've been pursued by a rifle shot ever since childhood. It was this shot that propelled me once and for all outside the realm of sleep. I was a child, and I slept with all the aptitude that children alone possess. The blast tore through the night and the world. I don't know how, in response, I managed to run down the length of the corridor: My little feet were rooted to the floor. In the living room, I found my father with his chest blown apart and his arms spread out in a sea of blood, as if he were swimming toward a shore only he could glimpse. In the midst of this world in collapse, my brother, Roland, remained seated in his room, the gun resting in his lap.

Don't touch me, he ordered, strangely calm. *Never touch me again. You'll burn.*

That's how he stayed, motionless, until relatives and neighbors burst into the house, panicking and shouting. From the window, I watched my brother being taken away by the police. There was no doubt about it: It was he who had shot our father, the respected hunter Henry Bullseye. An accident that our mother had already seen coming:

Firearms in the house only bring tragedy.

That was what Martina Bullseye used to say. On the day my father died, my mother was no longer there to witness her premonition. She had died some weeks before. A strange illness had consumed her in a trice. So at the tender age of ten—and in the space of a month—I became an orphan. And I was to be separated forever from my brother, Roland. As he was an adolescent, he was spared a police investigation. He was cleaning the gun, just as he often did, having been taught to do so by his father. And so they decided to take him to a psychiatric hospital. They say he never uttered another word; never again did he behave like a person. Roland was goodness incarnate but his mind was eclipsed, consumed by guilt. In the night sky of my mother's story, my brother joined the stars that had been swallowed up by the darkness.

My father was a man who filled the world—his foot would cross the threshold and we would feel the steadiness of his weight, as if we were in a little boat. What he did in life was far more than an occupation: Our father, the esteemed Henry Bullseye, was a hunter who was in great demand, and when he went away, he left our house full of sighs and mysteries. A tall, austere man, he was little given to talking. If I'd been cared for by him alone, I might never have learned to speak. My mother provided relief from this introverted side to my father: He was an emigrant from the mountains of Manica, where he had grown up among escarpments and rock faces. We would often hear his nostalgic yearning:

Where I was born, there's more earth than there is sky.

Maybe because he was from another tribe, Henry Bullseye chose a mulatto woman for a wife. At that time, it wasn't common for a black man to marry a woman from another race. The marriage made him even more solitary, driven out by blacks and excluded by whites and mulattoes. In fact, I only understood my old man when I became a hunter. My father was a stranger in his own world.

The receptionist at the newspaper offices is a fat woman, unhurried in speech and gesture. She seems to have been born like that, sitting, her backside like a planet competing with the Earth.

I've come to find out about the result of the contest.

I wave the clipping of the advertisement in front of the glass partition. The receptionist's shrill voice was made to seep out through the gaps in the broken glass:

Are you the hunter in person?

I'm the last of the hunters. And this is my last hunt.

The woman gazes up at the ceiling like an astronomer gazing up at the noonday sky. She opens an envelope in front of me, while I start talking again excitedly. She clearly wants to bide her time disclosing the result.

I don't know why they published the advertisement. There aren't any hunters anymore. There are people out there firing their guns. But they're not hunters. They're killers, every single one of them. And I'm the only hunter left.

Archangel Bullseye? Is that your name?

I'm the only one left, I repeat without answering her question. And I continue my feverish discourse. Soon, I assert, there won't be any animals left. For these false hunters spare neither the young nor pregnant females, they don't respect the closed season, they invade parks and reserves. Powerful people provide them with arms and whatever else they need.

It's all meat, it's all nhama, I say with a sigh, despondent.

Only then do I look again at the fat woman's expressionless eyes, as she waits for my disquisition to end.

Is your name Archangel Bullseye? Well, you're going to be able to hunt to your heart's content, you won the contest.

Can I come into your office? I want to give you a kiss.

With unexpected agility, the woman gets up, leans across the counter, and waits, her eyes closed, as if my kiss were the only prize she had won in her whole life.

I hurry away from the newspaper offices, dodging through the crowd of street vendors. I'm going to visit my brother, Roland, at the Infulene Psychiatric Hospital. He's been in the hospital ever since the accident in which our father lost his life. It's been a year since I last paid him a visit. Now I can't wait to tell him about the contest. Roland deserves to be the first to know. Besides, I don't have anyone else to share my happy news with.

It's a long bus ride. The hospital is quite a way beyond the suburban shanties. With my head leaning against the window, I watch crowds thronging the streets and sidewalks. Is there enough ground for so many people? And I hear my old man's lament: *Where I was born there's more earth than there is sky!* I close my eyes and, for a moment, I pretend that I come from somewhere else, full of earth and sky.

I sometimes ask myself whether I shouldn't be committed to the hospital as well. My brother's girlfriend, whose name is Luzilia, is a nurse and is convinced I'm mad. I don't argue—maybe I have gone mad. But then I ask: Can someone who no longer has a life also have his sanity? To tell you the truth, it was she, Luzilia, who made me lose my mind. It's because of her that I'm writing this diary, in the vain hope that this woman will one day read my muddled scrawl. Moreover, it's not the first time that I've embellished my handwriting for the sake of Luzilia. Once before, I addressed some brief but ill-fated lines to her. At the time, what I wrote was an invitation. What I'm scribbling now is my goodbye. A false farewell, like everything in a hunter's life, is a charade. Where for others there are memories, for me there are merely lies and illusions.

Luzilia is right: My madness began on the day a gunshot tore through my sleep and I discovered my father in the living room, spread-eagled in his own blood. Before I became an orphan, everything in me was intact: the house, time, the sky where I was told my mother was guarding the stars. All at once, however, I looked at life and got a fright: It was all so boundless and I was so small and so alone. Suddenly I stepped on the earth and re-coiled: My feet were so meager. All of a sudden there was nothing but the past: Death was a lake that was darker and more sluggish than the firmament. My mother was on the far shore, writing letters, while my father swam without ever crossing the endless waters.

Nothing has changed in the old hospital. It's Luzilia who comes to meet me in the large waiting room. She's still beautiful, her look seductive, the same habit of moistening her lips with her tongue. Luzilia is a nurse in that hospital—nothing there is strange to her.

It's so long since you were last here...

I've been so busy, one way or another, I lie.

Your brother and I got married.

I feign happiness. Luzilia talks and her voice recedes into the distance. She explains that Roland had been discharged the day before the wedding and they'd even tried living in her house. But it didn't work. Roland didn't know how to live outside his illness. And he was readmitted to the hospital.

I gradually stop listening to my brand-new relative. Perhaps I don't know how to be the brother-in-law of someone I wanted as a lover. I escape the present, returning to the events of a year before. It was in that same room that I confessed the deep love I felt for Luzilia. It was a long, empty afternoon, the type that spins out like some contagious disease. Without looking at her face, I took a deep breath and declared my love to the startled Luzilia. As she said nothing, I pressed ahead:

There's something I should say, Luzilia: Every time I come here to the hospital, it's you I come to see.

That's not true. What about your brother?

It's because of you that I come.

At this point I handed her a letter. Her little fingers remained still as she took her time reading it. Her hand lingered. Then she read in a low voice:

Ever since I started loving you, the whole world belongs to you. That's why I've never given you anything. I've merely returned things to you. I don't expect recompense. However, this message requests an answer. As tra-

dition dictates: If you love me, if my feelings are reciprocated, fold the corner of this letter and return it to me tomorrow.

The next day, Luzilia made no mention of the subject. She didn't bring the letter with her, and didn't say a word. She couldn't have imagined how wounded I was by her indifference. I should have contained myself, but was unable to:

So there's no fold in the letter?

She shook her head. I hid the hurt I felt at being rejected. For we do, indeed, have room enough to bury our little deaths deep within us! We travel down corridors, from one end to the other, in a silence that is as cold as that very asylum. As I left, Luzilia asked me:

Please don't stop coming to the hospital. Your brother has no one else.

You must throw my letter away.

I'll do that.

It was a stupid mistake to confess my feelings. I shouldn't have done it. So give me back the letter.

It's mine. Am I not mistress of everything?

One year later, and Luzilia walks in front of me, confirming her status as mistress of my soul, and owner of the world.

My brother, Roland, is sitting on the veranda of the infirmary, gazing, as always, at his own listless hands. It's as if time hasn't passed: There he is, surrendered, as ever, to his fate.

Tomorrow, I leave for the bush, I announce.

Nothing changes in him. He continues to look at his hands as if they were dead.

It's going to be my last hunt, I add.

At this point, his whole body stirs into action, in a sudden frenzy. My brother suddenly emerges from his enduring lethargy. With the despair of a man drowning, he leans on Luzilia's arm and approaches me. He seems to be talking, but he doesn't utter a word. He merely emits a kind of string of anxious sighs, as if swallowing more air than his chest can accommodate. The woman understands what he is trying to say, and nods in agreement. They understand each other. Then he returns to his old chair and sinks back into himself. As there's no more to be said, Luzilia accompanies me to the hospital gate. I'm the one to break the embarrassed silence.

What did Roland say?

He asked me to go with you on this hunting expedition.

Surely that can't be true!

Her eyes downcast, Luzilia makes a vague gesture, as if the whole thing were a nightmare.

Does he know something? I ask.

What do you mean?

About how I feel for you?

He's known that for a long time. Roland read your letter to me. He found it in my bag.

How could that be?

I never threw it away.

Roland suspected: My last hunt was a farewell to life. Even if I returned, safe and sound, to the city, I would never return to myself. Madness wasn't just a simple illness, but a family curse. And only hunting would save me from such a sickly fate.

This was the fear that Roland confessed to Luzilia. In his

despair, my brother was handing me a reason to go on clinging to life. This reason was the only woman he had ever loved. I turn my back, in a hurry to get away from the place, when Luzilia stops me:

Archie? Don't you want to know what I'd like to do?

No. It doesn't matter anymore. I don't want you to come, it's as simple as that. Your place is here, with Roland. Isn't that what you chose?

Mariamar's Version

TWO

Return from the River

A woman's true name is "Yes." Someone tells her: "You're not going." And she says, "I'm staying." Someone orders: "Don't talk." And she'll remain silent. Someone commands: "Don't do it." And she answers: "Very well."

—A PROVERB FROM SENEGAL

The night before, the order had been issued in our house: The women would remain shut away, far from those who would be arriving. Once again, we were excluded, kept apart, extinguished.

The following morning, I got down to the household chores. I wanted to give my mother a rest, for she had been lying, ever since the early morning, at the entrance to the yard. At one poi⟨⟩ I lay down next to her, determined to share with her some of ⟨⟩

burden of one who feels the weight of her soul. She took no notice of me at first. Then she mumbled between gritted teeth:

This village killed your sister. It killed me. Now it's never going to kill anyone again.

Please, Mother. We've just buried one of our own.

We women have been buried for a long time now. Your father buried me; your grandmother, your great-grandmother, they were all entombed alive.

Hanifa Assulua was right: Without knowing it, maybe I had been buried. So ignorant was I in matters of love, that I had been consigned to the grave. Our village was a living cemetery, only visited by its own residents. I looked at the houses that stretched out along the valley. Discolored, gloomy houses, as if they regretted emerging from the ground. Poor Kulumani, which never wanted to be a village. Poor me, who never wanted to be anything.

Time and again our mother had begged for us to go to the city.

I beseech you, husband, for the sake of all that is sacred: Let us go.

If you want to leave, then go.

We can leave someone to look after the graves.

It's the other way around, woman: If we leave, the graves will stop looking after us.

I shook off such memories. What point was there now in dwelling on past bitterness? If we clung so much to the past, how was it that Silência, so recently departed, could cause us to shed tears?

Father complains that yesterday, Mother, you ignored the requirements of those in mourning. Is it true that you offended the spirits?

Let me give you some advice, daughter: When you make love, do it in the river, in the water, as the fish do.

For God's sake, that isn't the kind of talk one expects from a mother!

Well, I'm telling you: Making love in the water is much better than in bed.

How do you know?

I watch our neighbor.

The neighbor? She can't, she's an out-and-out widow.

Smiling mischievously, she confessed: She would hide along the riverbank, and peer at the neighbor bathing all by herself. Little by little, that woman's hands would transform themselves into the hands of other creatures, and would strew her body with shivers that she'd never felt before.

Our neighbor taught me how to get my own back on men . . .

Did I understand what such a confession concealed? Our neighbor only made love to the dead. That's what Hanifa was telling me. Generation upon generation of the deceased had paraded through our neighbor's arms. People from afar, blue-blooded people, people who'd never been anything in life. All of them had their passions lit in her liquid bed. From all these lovers, each one chosen by her, the woman only reaped reward: There was no illness, no treachery, no risk of becoming pregnant. All that remained were memories, without ash or seed. Only far from the living could the women of Kulumani have their love reciprocated: That's what my mother taught me.

Your father's order is justified. From now on, you're not leaving the house.

I wasn't surprised that my father should want me to remain confined. What did puzzle me was the alacrity with which my mother supported her husband's decision.

*That's exactly what's going to happen, Mariamar: You're going to stay
here under lock and key.*

Then, I began to think: Perhaps I shouldn't be perplexed by
her determination to keep me away from the new arrivals. My
mother had not experienced love. The neighbor was the one
who'd been blessed: In her rivery bed, she had loved and been
loved. Conversely, Hanifa Assulua feared the road, travel, the
city. It wasn't my departure that worried her. It was the scorn
that might be leveled at her when no one wanted to take her
with them. Other mothers, elsewhere, would have wanted their
daughters to flourish out there in the world. But my family had
been contaminated by the pettiness that ruled over our village.

Those who came from outside, such as the imminent arrivals, would assume that the inhabitants of the village were good,
honest folk. This was an equally honest mistake. The people of
Kulumani are welcoming to those who are strangers and come
from far-off places. But among themselves, envy and malice pre-
vail. That's why our grandfather always reminded us:

We don't need enemies. To be beaten, all we need is ourselves.

The emptier one's life, the more it is peopled by those who've
already gone: the exiled, the insane, the dead. In Kulumani, we
all idolize the dead, for in them we preserve the deepest roots of
our dreams. The most senior of my dead relatives is Adjiru Kapitamoro. To be precise, he is my mother's elder brother. In our
region, we use the term "grandfather" to describe all our maternal uncles. In fact, Adjiru is the only grandfather I really knew.
At home, we called him *anakulu*, "our eldest." No one ever knew
is age, and not even he had any idea of when he had been born.

The truth is that he considered himself so everlasting that he claimed to have created the river that ran through our village.

I'm the one who made this river, the Lundi Lideia, he insisted haughtily.

The list of his fabulous fabrications was a long one: Apart from the river, Grandfather had also fashioned escarpments, chasms, and rain. All thanks to his powerful *mintela*, the mixtures and charms of the witch doctors. He, however, denied such a grandiose status:

I'm not a witch doctor, I'm just an old man.

In colonial times, his father, the revered Muarimi, had been appointed to the position of captain-major. He collected taxes and settled local disputes in favor of the colonists. This occupation made my great-grandfather the target for blame, envy, and lasting antipathy. But our family gained the name that it now bears proudly: We were the Kapitamoros. In a land without a flag, we hoisted this borrowed insignia as if it were our natural, time-honored right.

Contrary to family tradition, my grandfather Adjiru had embarked on a different pursuit: hunting. That is what he became, by vocation and calling: a hunter. *My arm is my soul*, he would say. He killed a man by accident as he hunted a leopard over Quionga way. In order to cleanse himself of this blood he would have to rub himself with the ash from burnt trees. He refused to take part in the ritual: For him, who considered himself Portuguese, such humiliation was unbearable. He was banned from hunting, and was limited to working as a tracker. He accepted this demotion with regal dignity. Until the day he died, he never lost his noble bearing. While his work meant that he stayed close the ground, he continued to cast his shadow over the whol

Kulumani. And now, as the village trembled at the threat of lions, everyone nostalgically recalled his divine protection.

My father, Genito Serafim Mpepe, could have been a hunter in his own right as well. But he preferred to remain a tracker, in a display of solidarity with his late mentor. If one had been demoted, the other had to be too. Genito's only ambition, in the end, was to follow in the footsteps of the dethroned hunter. Even so, Grandfather's standing proved impossible to equal. Adjiru had been more than a *mweniekaya*, the head of a family. His authority invariably extended to the entire neighborhood. Without pronouncements, his was a silent supremacy, that of someone who exercises power without need for words. As for me, Mariamar, I was a special person for him. Our "elder" reserved the most enigmatic of premonitions for me:

You, Mariamar, came from the river. And you will surprise everyone yet: One day you'll go there where the river goes, he prophesied.

I'm a woman, and it could never be my destiny to travel. Yet Adjiru Kapitamoro was right. For only two days after Silência's funeral, I'm traveling downstream in a skiff. I'm fleeing the custody imposed by my inveterate jailer, Genito Mpepe. To escape from Kulumani, there's no road and no bush. My father's on the road. In the bush, there are the killer lions. At each exit, an ambush awaits. The only way left to me is the river. This thread of water was baptized with the name Lideia, after the doves that visit us in the rainy season. It could perfectly well have remained an anonymous little river, but we feared that if it was left nameless, might become extinguished forever. It was supposedly our ndfather, Adjiru Kapitamoro, who had given it its name. And retended we believed it.

So here we both go: the River Lideia with its bird's name; and I, Mariamar, with my watery name. I travel against my fate, but with the flow of the river's current. During this whole time, the skiff feigns obedience. It's not my arms that propel it along but forces that I would rather remained unknown. November is the month when we pray for rain. And I pray for a land where I can lie down with the rain, weightless and freed from my body.

They say that farther on, this river flows through the city. I doubt it. This river of mine, which doesn't even speak Portuguese, this river full of fish that only know their names in Shimakonde, I don't believe it would be allowed into the city. And I'll be stopped as well if I get as far as knocking on the door of the capital.

Obey everything except love, that's what my poor sister Silência used to say. It's for reasons of love that I'm leaving Kulumani, putting distance between me and myself, my present fears, my future nightmares. It's not so much the desire to break my ties that has led me to disobey. I have another, more important reason: I've embarked on this act of madness because of the visitors' reported arrival. In fact, because of one such arrival: Archangel Bullseye, the hunter. That man once hunted me. Ever since then, I've had no peace. To flee from a lover is the most complete act of obedience to him. The more I'm mistress of my fate, the more I'm a slave to that love of mine. There's no river in this world that can free me from this trap.

Archie Bullseye came into my life sixteen years ago. I was also sixteen years old when he first met me. I was no more tha young girl, but my eyes had aged more than my body. My only ambition was to run far away from Kulumani. On Sunday afternoons I would break into the henhouse of the Catholic Mission to sell chickens out on the highway. My intention was to make a bit of money so that I could run away to the city. But the road was almost deserted, with very few travelers. It was 1992, and the war had finished that same year, but an invisible garrote continued to asphyxiate our area.

I never understood why so many vendors would crowd together on the edge of the lifeless road. Maybe they were gathered there in a type of prayer, a way of kneeling together before our fate. Or perhaps it was because the occasional furtive timber truck would appear. Such businesses belonged to powerful people, whom we called "the owners of the land." But whoever passed by, I would hold my chickens up and their wings would flutter blindly, in momentary flight. No one ever stopped, no one ever bought anything. Clucking stupidly, the fowl would once again dangle from my hands, as if burdened by their daring effort to be birds but a few moments before.

Once, the policeman, Maliqueto Próprio—the only representative of the law in Kulumani—came up to me, all self-important, wanting to know where I'd got my merchandise. He pointed to the chickens as if they were proof of a crime. He charged me with theft, and ordered me to follow him.

To the police station? I asked, shaking.

You know very well there's no police station in Kulumani. I've got my own lockup.

Maliqueto's abuses were only too well known. At that moment, his sinister look merely confirmed his malicious intentions. My eyes failed me and my legs wobbled. The barrel of his n sticking into my back didn't permit any delay.

Please don't do me any harm.

That was when Archangel Bullseye appeared, like a hero emerging from nowhere. He stopped in front of me, mounted on his motorbike, a proud emperor and a man whose orders the world respected. The policeman eyed the intruder, measuring him from head to foot. After a ponderous silence, he decided to withdraw. I don't know whether the hunter was aware of the opportunity that his appearance had presented him with, but he smiled as he interjected:

Can I take a chicken?

It was me I wanted him to take. The man looked at me with apparent surprise. Suddenly I felt the weight of shame: I had never been looked at before. It was as if at long last my body were being born within me.

Those eyes, he sighed. *Ah! Those eyes!*

My face fell and I stood there confused, a bird with neither flight nor voice.

You have a lovely body, the visitor murmured.

His talk laid bare both my body and soul. To escape my unsteadiness, I retreated to some shade by the river. The man followed me, pushing his motorbike.

Would you like to come to Palma with me?

The town? I can't.

I'll take you there and bring you back on the bike. We can take a shortcut along the river so that no one will see us.

I can't, I've already told you.

We can watch television, wouldn't you like that?

I contemplated the surrounding countryside. How vast the world was, how infinitely vast! The universe was immense and the visitor was waiting for an answer. So many things went through my head! It occurred to me, for instance, to ask the hunter to help my mother carry water if he had a motorbike. To help the women of Kulumani to fetch firewood, dig clay, transport crops from their allotments. And above all, not to ask anything of me.

We stood in silence as my eyes lingered over the waters of the Lideia. Tired of waiting, Archie asked the name of the river. He said that he was coming to hunt a savage crocodile that was spreading terror in the area. He wasn't going to do anything without knowing the river's name.

I sighed. The visitor didn't want to know my name. Only the landscape seemed to interest him.

Lundi Lideia, that's its full name, I replied begrudgingly. *But we just call it the Lideia.*

So what does it mean?

Lideia is the name we give to a type of dove.

A dove? Archie pondered. Then he laughed, finding a joke where I could see none.

Fair enough! There are rivers that make us fly.

Those were the hunter's words. We said goodbye while looking at the river, that same river that I'm now using to get away from Kulumani, to escape from my family, and break out of my own life.

When, in the early hours, I threw myself into this journey, it was my intention to warn the hunter of the ambush that was being mounted against him. My plan was straightforward: I would jump out of the skiff by the bridge and set off down the highway, where I would wait for the visitors. Sixteen years ago, Archie had saved me from the threat of a lewd policeman. This time, I'd be the one to save him. And I could see myself standing in the middle of the road, my arms waving like flags fluttering. Who knows, maybe the hunter would take me in his arms and bear me aloft in giddy flight.

But while I am carried down the river, another sentiment takes hold of me. I'm not going to meet the hunter. Rather, I'm fleeing from him. Why am I running away from the only person who might have loved me? I don't know how to answer. My mother often says that water makes the stones round in the same way that women shape the souls of men. It could have been like that with me. But it wasn't. There was no love, no man, no soul. What happened was that with the passing of time, I lost all hope. And when someone stops having hopes, it's because they've stopped living. So that's why I'm running away: I fear being devoured. Not by the anxiety that dwells deep within me. Devoured by the emptiness of not loving. Devoured by the desire to be loved.

The skiff arrives, at last, at a pool of clear water. This pool is considered a sacred spot, which only witch doctors dare visit. In the village, it is said that it's here that the water makes its nest. The older folk call this place *lyali wakati*, the "egg of time." The peace and quiet of this paradise ought to mollify me, but it doesn't. Because I realize that the skiff is stuck, and despite all my efforts, I can't move on. There's no sign of a current, no sign of an eddy. But the skiff is stuck fast on the bed of the River Lideia. It must be fulfilling the age-old rule: Small places have a wide reach. No matter how hard we try to leave, we never get away. *What a cursed land, so devoid of sky that we even have to exhume the clouds*, was what Grandfather Adjiru would complain. And that's how I now execrate my native land.

A tremor shakes me, my heart leaps up through my throat when, standing up in my unsteady skiff, I sense a hidden presence on the riverbank. Although I'm a woman, I have inherited the hunter's instinct that runs through my family. I know of shadows that move among shadows, I know of smells and signs that no one else knows about. And now I'm certain: There's an animal on the riverbank! There's a creature creeping furtively through the foliage next to the water.

And suddenly, there it is: a lioness! She's come down to drink from the calm water on that part of the riverbank. She contemplates me without fear or excitement. As if she had been waiting for me for a long time, she raises her head and pierces me with her inquisitive gaze. There is no tension in her behavior. It might be said that she recognizes me. More than this: The lioness greets me with a sisterly respect. We linger in this mutual contemplation and, gradually, a sense of spiritual harmony takes hold of me.

Having slaked her thirst, the lioness stretches as if she wanted a second body to emerge from her own. Then she slowly withdraws, her tail swaying like a furry pendulum, each step caressing the earth's surface. I smile with uncontained pride. They are all convinced that it is male lions who are threatening the village. It's not. It's this lioness, delicate and feminine as a dancer, majestic and sublime as a goddess, it's this lioness that has spread such terror through the neighborhood. Powerful men, warriors equipped with sophisticated weapons: All of them have prostrated themselves, enslaved by fear, vanquished by their own impotence.

Once again, the lioness fixes her gaze upon me, and then turns in a circle before disappearing. Something that I shall never be able to describe suddenly robs me of my good judgment and a shout bursts from my breast:

Sister! My sister!

In despair, my fists grasp the oars in an attempt to propel the skiff toward the shore:

Silência! Uminha! Igualita!

The names of my dead sisters reverberate through that mysterious setting. I shiver from head to foot: I had just challenged the sacred precepts that forbade me from uttering the names of the dead. Attracted by their summons, the deceased may reappear in the world. Perhaps that was my secret wish. A desperate urge causes me to disobey the rule once more:

It's me, sister, it's me, Mariamar!

I then realize how absurd my situation is: I, who had never raised my voice, was now shouting for someone who could not hear. They're right, the people who point a finger at me: I'm mad, I've lost control of myself. And I burst into tears, as if I were suddenly aware of how little I cried when I was born. Adjiru was right: Sadness isn't crying. Sadness is having no one to cry for.

Don't leave me, please, take me with you.

The call echoes through the forest, and for a second I seem to hear other voices clamoring for Silência. But the vegetation closes in on itself, thick and unmoving. In the place where the lioness has just drunk, there's now a red stain rapidly spreading across the surface of the water. Suddenly the whole river has turned red, and I am drifting in blood. The same blood that, every time I dreamed of giving birth, would flow out between my thighs, the same blood that is now flowing in the current. My grandfather, Adjiru Kapitamoro, was right: This river was born from his hands, just as I was born from his attachment to me.

And at this point, I understand: More than the land, my prison was my grandfather Adjiru. It was he who had brought the skiff to a standstill and held me back in the Lideia's sacred pool.

Grandfather, I plead. *Please let me continue downstream.*

I curl up in the bottom of the skiff, I lie there seeking the sleep of those who are not yet born. Then, all of a sudden, another skiff penetrates the silence and, to my alarm, approaches me like some furtive crocodile. It can only be Adjiru coming to rescue me. With a tight throat, I call out:

Grandfather?

The two craft are now alongside each other and a figure leans over me to tie a rope round the oarlocks of my boat. The light is behind this intruder, and all I can see is a dark silhouette. Not wanting to waste time, I point to the shore and declare:

She was there! The lioness was there. Let's follow her, Grandfather, she can't have got far.

Sit up, Mariamar.

I am startled: It's not Adjiru. It's Maliqueto Próprio, the village's solitary hangman. Without uttering a word, he starts dragging me back toward Kulumani. Halfway, he ships his oars and stares fixedly at me until the abandoned boat begins to glide away downstream at the whim of the current.

You owe me something, Mariamar. Have you forgotten? This is a good place to pay me your debt.

He starts taking off his clothes, while crawling toward me, slithering and slobbering. Funnily enough, I'm not scared of him. To my own surprise, I advance toward Maliqueto, my hackles raised, screaming, spitting, and scratching. Between alarmed and astonished, the policeman retreats and looks with horror at the deep gashes I've inflicted on his arms.

You great bitch, were you trying to kill me?

He pulls his shirt up over his shoulders in order to hide his wounds and hurriedly resumes the journey back to Kulumani. As he rows, he keeps repeating under his breath:

She's crazy, the hag's completely crazy.

On the shore, Florindo Makwala, the administrator, and my father, Genito Mpepe, are waiting. In anticipation, I start shouting, although my voice is thickened by the tension:

I saw it, I saw it! It was the lioness, Father! And it was real. I didn't make it up.

You're lying. Don't come to me with stories, because I'm going to punish you.

I saw it, Father. A lioness at the pool. I'm sure as sure can be.

Maliqueto, contradicting me for the sake of it, insists that there was nothing to see there. And even if I had seen it, how could I be sure it was a female? In this area, male lions are small and almost without a mane.

The district officer steps forward with care so as not to get his shoes wet, and, keeping himself at a distance, instructs my father:

I don't want any contact between this girl and the delegation.

She'll be kept at home, rest assured, Comrade Chief. I'll tie her up in the yard.

I want her kept well away from the visitors. And what's happened to you, Maliqueto? Are you bleeding?

I hurt myself with the ropes, Chief. And now, with your permission, can I say something, Chief?

Go ahead.

Your daughter was wrong in the head, Comrade Mpepe, but now she's scary. How did she dare visit that sacred place all by herself?

You're right, Maliqueto. Don't you know what they did to Tandi, who went where she wasn't supposed to go?

The three men busy themselves with securing the boat. Sitting on the riverbank, I realize how similar the skiff is to a coffin. The bulging belly, the same journey toward timelessness. The river didn't take me to my destination. But the journey led me to someone who had become separated from me: the lioness, the sister I missed so much.

The Hunter's Diary

TWO

The Journey

My butterfly net is held aloft, and I merely wait for the butterfly to prompt me through its withdrawals and its hesitations. How happy I would be if I could dissolve into light and air, merely in my quest to get close and dominate it. The old law of the hunt plants itself between me and my prey: the more I try and obey the animal with all my being, the more I transform myself in body and soul into a butterfly. The nearer I get to fulfilling my hunter's desire, the more this butterfly gains human form and volition. In the end, it is as if this capture were the price I have to pay in order to regain my human existence... Returning from the hunt, the spirit of the doomed creature takes possession of the hunter.

—FROM "BUTTERFLY HUNT," BY WALTER BENJAMIN

I've never liked airports. So full of people, so full of no one. I prefer train stations, where there's enough time for tears and waving handkerchiefs. Trains set off sluggishly, with a sigh, regretting their departure. But a plane has a haste that's inhuman. And my mother's story loses any meaning when I watch planes hurtling into the air. Not everything, after all, is so slow in the endless firmament. I'm at Maputo International Airport, certain that I'm nowhere at all. Someone speaking in English brings me back to earth.

This is the writer. He's going to be your travel companion.

The writer is a white man, short, with beard and glasses. He's a well-known intellectual, and various people stop to ask him for his autograph. He gets up to shake my hand.

I'm Gustavo. Gustavo Regalo.

He seems to like his own name. He is waiting for me to show recognition. But I pretend he's a complete stranger.

I'm going to write a report on the hunting expedition. I'm under contract to the same company as you.

I'm sure you'll enjoy it. And the lions will be pleased to know that their deaths warrant a report.

This is my first hunt. I have to say, without meaning any offense, that I'm against it.

Against what?

Against hunting. All the more so when it's hunting lions.

Your problem, my writer friend, is that you've never seen a lion.

What do you mean by that?

You've seen lions in photos of safaris, but you don't know what a lion is. A lion only really reveals himself in territory where he's lord and king. Join me in the bush and you'll know what a lion is.

Four hours in a plane, seated next to the writer, are enough to gauge the abyss that separates us. With his intellectual airs, his notepad at the ready, his inability to keep quiet: In short, the writer irritates me. Judging by the way he looks at me, I realize that the reverse is also true. Something about him reminds me of Roland and the way my brother used to contemplate me. As if he were accusing me.

A feather is heavy; a bird is also heavy. The lightest knows how to fly. So goes my late mother, Dona Martina's saying. Well, as far as I'm concerned, both lightnesses are heavy, and my sleep never turns into nocturnal flight. A constant state of alertness makes me enter and leave sleep like a drunkard, makes me come and go like a shipwrecked sailor. It's a legacy of that fateful night when Roland shot my father. Insomnia brings back unwelcome memories; sleeping washes away memories I wanted to keep. Sleep is my illness, my madness.

During the journey, I feel an overwhelming lethargy. I pretend to be asleep in order to then pretend I'm woken up by the tearing of a sheet of paper. Gustavo apologizes, smiling timidly:

I'm going to write my girlfriend a letter. In the old style. A fake letter just to distract myself, to distract myself from missing her.

A fake letter? Is there any letter that isn't a fake? I remember the love letters that my father would dictate to my mother. It was a late evening ritual, when one could hear the frogs croaking in the nearby ponds. We were blacks and mulattoes who had been demoted to blacks. We were restricted to the edge of the area, there where rains and illness accumulated. Martina Bullseye, my mother, would beautify herself for these writing sessions, for they were the only time when she would receive compliments from her man. It was only at such moments that he behaved in a mild, almost submissive manner, as if he were asking for forgiveness. Sitting motionless, bent over the paper, my mother looked like some aged canvas. Next to her, Roland scribbled endless pieces of homework. At that moment, he was even older than our own mother. Even today I can remember my father's voice vividly, as he dictated, enunciating every syllable:

My darling Henry, my beloved husband, one and only love of my life... Are you writing this down, Martina?

He would dictate long letters that were always the same. In doing so, he would roll his words with slow deliberation, as if he were drunk. What a difficult relationship Father had with words! I inherited that problematic relationship with the written word, in contrast to Roland, for whom letters were a game with which to play. Maybe that's why I'm irritated by the fluency with which my traveling companion keeps scribbling line after line. Or who knows, perhaps what perturbs me is that I don't have anyone to write a love letter to.

The writer has finished his imaginary letter, and folds the paper carefully so as to slip it into an envelope. He zips open his briefcase and places it inside, among various other envelopes. The letter may be a fake, but the performance is a convincing one. And, once again, I'm assailed by a memory. Far from us, Henry Bullseye would complete the same ritual: He would invariably place the letter in an envelope, lick the flap and stick it down, and put it in his travel bag. He would take those letters on his lengthy hunting expeditions. He also carried with him a blurred photograph of Martina.

It's like that so that others can see it, but can't look too hard.

He was a jealous man, old Henry! In fact his jealousy became a reason for bloodletting and tragedy.

Through the window of the plane, the last signs of daylight dissolve among the clouds. I recall my mother's fable condemning the Sun for its petulance and the way I, maybe because of this story, always feel myself awakening as darkness begins to fall. I belong to neither day nor night. Sunset was the time when I would return home, exhausted from my endless games in those backyards that opened up like a vast savanna where my imagination hunted its prey. Roland would look at me, jealous of my intimacy with the world. Roland belonged to the house. I belonged to the street.

Mother, please don't make me have a bath yet. Let me stay dirty for just a bit longer.

The sweat and dust that covered me prolonged the rapture of my forests invented in the back gardens of the neighborhood. As my father was almost always absent, Martina Bullseye was able to exercise her mother's complacency with sovereign freedom. What came as a relief to us seemed to weigh heavily on her heart. During those long periods of solitude, our mother would continue to fulfill the ritual of those commissioned letters: She would put on her most elegant dress—in fact, the only dress she possessed—and pretend to listen to the absent Henry Bullseye's dictation. She performed the act of writing with such devotion that we could clearly hear our father's slow drawl echoing down the hallway.

Why are we going so fast?

The writer doesn't answer. Ever since the plane landed in Pemba, we have begun a long journey by road to Palma, the district capital. We can look forward to a nine-hour drive along poorly maintained sandy roads.

There are four people in the all-terrain vehicle: in front, myself and Gustavo, the writer; in the back, Florindo Makwala, the district administrator, and his outsized spouse, Dona Naftalinda. The First Lady, as the administrator insists on calling her, justifies her name: She is so heavy that the vehicle has developed a dangerous list on the side where she is sitting.

Gustavo is the driver. I chose to remain free to watch the bush that lines the road. For the last two hours, the scenery has been no more than a monotonous procession of scrawny, bare trees, devoid of foliage.

Why such speed? I ask again.

The question has become an order. Gustavo needs to be aware of who is leading this expedition. We are two opposites. The writer is white and short. I'm a mulatto and tall. The writer shoots his mouth off and looks at people right in the eye. On the contrary, the human eye robs me of my soul; the more human the gaze, the more of an animal I become.

Is there still far to go? Gustavo asks, mumbling so low that no one hears him.

At last, the man complies: The car slows down while I give him a smile of unconcealed scorn. I glance over at the rear seat.

Are you asleep, Dona Naftalinda?

Her silence is in concert with the surrounding countryside: It's as if the world were yet to be born. Inside the car, the hush is even heavier. I know that silence and the way, on very hot days, it sinks into us. It begins by inhibiting our very desire to talk. Later, we've even forgotten what it was we wanted to say. Before long, even the act of breathing becomes a waste of energy.

Archie's right, drive more slowly, Dona Naftalinda complains. *The road's in a shocking state, and we're being thrown around in the back.*

Naftalinda's tone is adjusted to her status: It has the geniality of someone who knows so well what she wants that she has no need to issue a command. My gaze ranges over the landscape like fire licking the elephant grass. Where the writer sees trees, I see places to shelter made out of shadows. In one of these shadows, the ill-famed lions, eaters of people and of dreams, will be resting.

So absorbed am I reviewing the shadows that I am unaware of a lively monologue that has begun from the direction of the backseat. The administrator is rattling on about automobiles, makes, models, countries of origin, and the years in which his favorite vehicles were manufactured. And how he could do with an automobile like this one provided by the company that contracted us.

Is there still far to go? I ask, merely to change the subject.

The administrator repeats what he has already said a dozen times: Not far at all. In fact we're almost there. The writer asks:

It's strange, one doesn't see any people around. Doesn't anyone live here?

Florindo Makwala stiffens, offended. Was the visitor suggesting that all he ruled over were stones and dust?

You'll see them in a little while. The people. There are lots of them.

———

Stop, stop the car! I order, the door already open and half of me outside the vehicle. The next minute, I creep over toward some bushes on the side of the road. There are vultures circling high above. Maybe there's a rotting corpse somewhere around here. It's a false alarm. I signal the others to get out of the vehicle.

Let's take a break.

Dona Naftalinda is lowered from the vehicle. The long-suffering jeep's suspension groans. The anxious administrator warns:

Help her down. Don't let her fall, for God's sake don't let her fall.

Don't you dare touch me, husband. Don't forget it's forbidden.

Various arms are raised to help in the operation to unload the First Lady. I hesitate, unsure where to place my hands. I'm afraid my arms will get lost among folds and rolls of fat. In front of me, a huge backside darkens the day, like a sudden eclipse of the sun.

If I'd known, I would have brought a crane, the writer murmurs in my ear.

Once on the ground, Naftalinda whispers something to her husband. The administrator mutters awkwardly between his teeth.

My wife needs to go into the bush.

She can go, I answer curtly.

She's scared.

Go with her.

She would rather you kept guard over her.

In these, as in other matters, it's better if the husband does that.

It's not that I'm scared, Naftalinda declares, with the air of an empress. *But I've heard that the lions only kill women. I don't know whether, as First Lady, I'm also included on their menu.*

You can be sure that you are, the writer comments.

Over there's safe, I assure her, pointing to some rocks in front of us. *You can go, Dona Naftalinda, we'll watch over things from here.*

To distract ourselves from our embarrassing wait, the writer pretends to become interested in my rifle and admits:

There was a time when I dreamed of using a gun; I wanted to be a guerrilla fighter. In those days, we used to say that freedom would be born from the barrel of a gun.

So did it happen?

Freedom?

No. I'm asking whether you became a guerrilla.

More or less.

There's no more or less when it comes to guns and freedom. Have you ever seen anyone get killed?

Never. And you? Have you ever killed someone, or has it always just been animals?

I am immediately struck by the memory of my father swimming in blood that wasn't just his own, but that of all the Bullseyes. My words are rendered more somber by my solemn tone. Those we have killed, no matter whether they are strangers to us or our enemies, become members of our family forever after. They never leave us, but remain more present than the living.

Returning to our company once more, Dona Naftalinda smiles, amused by the way the writer shakes the dust from himself as if in some act of self-flagellation.

See the advantage of being a lion? A lion never gets himself dirty, Dona Naftalinda asserts.

All I want is a bath. I've got more dust on me than I have clothes, Gustavo complains, shaking himself vigorously.

So much the better, I advise him in a sarcastic tone. *You're much better off like that because your body will begin to get used to the land. Get used to being part of the land, belonging to this land.*

I am of this land.

Only the land can confirm that.

I turn my back and walk away, though not before I hear the writer mutter angrily to himself:

Arrogant bastard!

When we get back to the car, the administrator hurries to inspect our cargo: Ten goats are squeezed into the baggage compartment. The creatures appear calm, displaying the stupid good humor of ruminants.

Wouldn't it be better to tether them? Dona Naftalinda asks.

The goats had spent the whole journey standing, balancing themselves with professional skill, like a troupe of dancers. Florindo comments proudly: A goat was made to ride in a car, it can keep its balance even over an abyss, where there's no longer any ground. Then the administrator opens his arms in a gesture of friendship:

Don't forget, Comrade Hunter: One of these animals is for you to use as bait for the lion. Choose the one you want.

There must be some mistake here, my dear administrator. A number of mistakes, for that matter: In the first place, I'm not your comrade. But what's more important is the fact that I don't hunt with bait. I'm a hunter, not a fisherman.

Do as you wish. But the truth is this: Whether you're fishing or hunting, you've got to eliminate these lions. It's one of my political objectives.

The eaters of people are a political matter as far as he is concerned.

My superiors, he reminds us emphatically, *gave very clear instructions: The people have the vote, animals don't. The reason behind this community's complaints must be eradicated.* And he repeats his per-functory order: *You've got to kill them.*

I won't kill them. Of that you can be sure, I reply.

What's that you're saying?

I'm a hunter. I don't kill, I hunt.

Isn't that the same thing, surely?

For you, it may be. For me, it's completely different. But let me say one thing before we get to the village. I wasn't recruited by the administration. My only obedience is to whoever is paying me.

We set off again on our journey, and all of a sudden a cloud of dust once more disturbs the timeless peace of the savanna. The administrator realizes he should retreat from his confrontation with me. The presence of a well-known writer is a unique op-portunity for him to polish his image. In an offhand way, he af-firms, as if he were thinking out loud:

Whether you're killing or hunting, what's important is that people can return to their daily activities. In their struggle to overcome absolute poverty.

The man is no longer talking. He's giving a speech. And he declares that the expedition, led by his party, will save people condemned to poverty. He uses that grand word: "save." In the car mirror, I watch the dust disperse and I'm overcome by a gentle drowsiness: How I'd like to be saved! How I'd like to wallow, like a drowning man, in the arms of a savior. Or, to be more precise: in Luzilia's arms.

When you go hunting, I'll go with you, Comrade Archie, the adminis-trator declares.

In hunting, no one goes with anyone, I reply. *In hunting, there are only two creatures: the one who kills and the one who dies.*

I need my people to see me, to see me returning to the village with the trophy.

At last, some houses come into view.

Not long now, Naftalinda tells the writer, *and people will come out onto the road in their droves.*

Those aren't people living in those houses, the administrator clarifies.

They're not people living there? Gustavo asks. *Who lives there, then?*

It's fear that lives there, he replies.

Nine hours after leaving Pemba, the capital of the province, our delegation arrives at the village. The administrator was right. But it's not just fear that inhabits Kulumani. Terror is etched into the faces of the crowd that surrounds us.

Don't stop the vehicle in the middle of the road, Makwala orders.

I smile. The road is so narrow that it has no middle. Nor does it have shoulders: Everything on either side has gained the color of dust. I too am so covered in dust that it's as if my body is the same on the inside and the outside. I shake myself down, and my hands are clouds that seem to have migrated from my body. My chest is shaken by a fit of coughing. Some nebulous entity seems to be taking charge of me.

Unaware of all this, a sea of people envelops us. The administrator's wife whispers an explanation in my ear: All the country folk from the surrounding villages have been mobilized to come and welcome us. Defying all the rules about safety, these villagers will march back to their homes at night. But it all seems inevitable: A chief's strength is measured by the welcome he's given. And Florindo Makwala doesn't want to pass up a chance to impress us. He doesn't allow the credits to escape him as he openly encourages Gustavo Regalo:

See, my dear Regalo? The people love us. Me and my party. Write all this down, take photos of it all.

In the middle of the throng someone grabs my arm. I reciprocate, clumsily shaking his hand. Then I notice that he's blind. It was his stray gesture that collided with me and caused me to stop in my tracks. He's wearing camouflaged military fatigues that stand in contrast to his bare feet.

You people have arrived! the blind man exclaims, as if we were fulfilling our destiny. And then he proclaims: *You have come to shed your blood in Kulumani.*

All of a sudden I give in to a strange impulse and start waving at the crowd. I remember other occasions when I've been received as a savior. But these people are looking at me obliquely. The blind man's clammy hand seizes my arm once again:

Have you brought a rifle? What for? These lions aren't going to be killed with a bullet.

The vigor with which he pursues me makes me doubt the truth of his blindness. My suspicion grows stronger when he grabs me with the despair of one struggling for breath and asks me:

Can you see me?

Why do you ask?

No one can see us, the people of Kulumani, only the muwavi, *the witch doctors, pay us any attention.*

The administrator helps free me from the blind man's intrusiveness. He pushes me to the front of the vehicle, where the headlights have opened up a patch of light, and whispers:

We've arrived at night. Some of them think we are vashilo.

Who?

Vashilo, *people of the night. We're the only ones visiting villages at this hour.*

Then the administrator issues an order in a loud voice:

Let them by! We've come to save you, we've brought with us someone to kill the lions.

The blind man bows respectfully and once again leans on my arm before concluding:

There's no dying, there's no killing. You've all come to die here in our abode.

I look around me. Two nights ago, a young woman was killed here. Before her, some twenty others were eaten by the creatures of the wild. Not far away, in the middle of the long grass, there might still be blood-soaked tracks, the indelible relics of unspeakable crimes. I think of the pain and the terror of these people. I think of the helplessness of this village, so far from the world and from God. Kulumani was more of an orphan than I.

Night has fallen—there are no more shadows in the world.

Mariamar's Version

THREE

An Unreadable Memory

> Every morning the gazelle wakes up knowing that it has to run more swiftly than the lion or it will be killed. Every morning the lion awakens knowing that it has to run faster than the gazelle or it will die of hunger. It doesn't matter whether you're a lion or a gazelle: When the Sun rises, you'd better start running.
>
> —AFRICAN PROVERB

Last night, when the strangers arrived in Kulumani, I didn't make a point of watching their reception in front of the administration building. I could have escaped my confinement for a few moments. But I didn't even bother. For years, my reason for living had been the dream of seeing Archie Bullseye again. Now there he was, just a few steps away, and I remained distant and withdrawn, peering out at the crowd milling around the visiting delegation. They were like vultures. They were feeding on leftovers. What was left of ourselves. And that's what I told my mother: *They're like vultures.* And birds of prey, according to local wisdom, don't lose their sight even after they've died.

Hanifa Assulua's authoritarian voice brought me down to earth: *Stop sleeping in the shelter of your eyelashes, Mariamar! Go and throttle a chicken.*

A huge feast is being prepared to welcome the visitors. We women will remain in the shadows. We wash, sweep, cook, but none of us will sit down at the table. My mother and I know what we have to do, almost without exchanging a word. My job is to go and catch, kill, and pluck a chicken from our henhouse. As it evades me in a noisy, headlong rush, I hear footsteps behind me, as if someone were joining the chase. I stop running and, with bated breath, my eyes sweep the ground, searching anxiously. I can't see anyone, and an anguished sigh escapes my breast:

Is that you, sister?

Eventually I realize I'm alone, sitting on the steps up to the chicken coop, where the chickens spend the night safe from the animals that prey on them.

Somewhere, so near here, Archie Bullseye is staying. And here am I, in the empty yard, plucking the chicken between my knees. The feathers flutter away, carried on the gentle breeze. Suddenly I glimpse Silência, in silhouette against the light, gathering up the floating feathers in her hands. She cups her hands so that nothing can slip away between her fingers and presents me with this soft, downy offering. I accept the gift and hear her familiar voice:

See here, sister: This is my heart. The lions didn't take it. You know whom you should give it to.

I notice blood running down my arms, my *capulana*, my legs. Surely it's the blood of the chicken, that's what it looks like, but giddiness stops me from seeing properly. An uncontrollable rage bursts from my breast, a volcanic eruption. Then I hear my mother's voice coming from the house:

Come on, Mariamar, haven't you killed the chicken yet? Or are you plucking shadows as usual?

I try to answer, but words fail me. All of a sudden I've lost the power of speech, and my chest is convulsed by no more than a hoarse croak. Alarmed, I jump to my feet, I run my hands down my neck, across my mouth and face. I scream for help but can only emit a cavernous roar. And it's at that moment that I get the awaited sensation: a sandy scraping across the roof of my mouth, as if I'd suddenly been fitted with the tongue of a cat. Hanifa Assulua appears at the door, hands on hips, expectantly:

Having another fit, Mariamar?

Mother's appearance scares Silência. I hear her steps receding quickly, hurrying away while the anxious sound of clucking makes me certain that the chickens also felt her presence. They hadn't realized that one of them lay lifeless on my lap. But they recognized the furtive movement of our dead visitor. If it's true that I'm mad, then I share my madness with the birds.

My mother comes nearer, curious. Slowly, she draws her hands up to her face as if seeking help. Then, a few feet away, she stops, horrified:

What have you done to the chicken? Didn't you use the knife, girl?

Mother turns her back, disconcerted, and makes for the shelter of the house. I look at the chicken, torn to pieces, spread out across the ground. That's when I see a vulture land at my feet.

At that moment, I recall an episode from the past: When the priests withdrew from Kulumani at the height of the war, there was no one to look after the aviary at the mission. The chickens were abandoned in their coops, which began to fall apart. Little by little, the birds became wild, scratching around persistently in the open ground and only returning to the henhouses at night. The chicken coops gradually disintegrated, and the old wooden boards disappeared, eaten away by termites. This was a warning: The border between order and chaos was being erased. The primordial savanna was coming to reclaim what had been stolen from it.

And that's what happened: The chickens were devoured, one at a time, by the vultures. The birds of prey occupied the space previously reserved for domestic fowl, and made themselves so much at home that they lost all fear of us. Half a dozen of them eventually obeyed Grandfather Adjiru's call, and he, as a reward, would toss them a few chunks of fat.

One time, dinner was pompously announced in our house.

It's chicken today, what are we celebrating?

We were suspicious of the size of the roasted bird. Only I had the courage to express my doubts:

Are we eating vulture?

And what if we are? my father retorted. *Have you never heard it said that we hunters eat the eyes of vultures so as to gain their pinpoint vision?*

I never found out what I ate. But the truth is that ever since that meal, I never again got a good night's sleep. Nightmares tore me from my bed and I would awaken with unwanted cravings, a greed that stole away my very being. The manner in which such hunger took possession of me was not human. To tell the truth, I didn't just feel hunger. I was hunger from head to foot, and my mouth watered viscous saliva.

It's early morning and you're still eating the leftovers from dinner? What sort of hunger is this? my grandfather, ever an early riser, asked, bewildered.

I was taken to Palma for some tests at the hospital. *It could be diabetes,* the nurse ventured. The suspicion was groundless. None of the tests revealed any illness and I returned to Kulumani without any relief from the mysterious fits.

In the early morning, my grandfather continued to pass me on the veranda while I was scratching around among the remains of dinner, picking out chicken bones from the manioc flour. Adjiru took advantage of the darkness to exercise his other activity: that of carving masks. In accordance with ancestral precepts, this was a secret task, and no one could suspect that the masks were fashioned by his hands. These carvings invariably portrayed women: The goddesses we once were didn't want to be forgotten. The hands of men uttered that which their mouths dared not speak.

Can I make a mask? I asked.

A mask, he said, isn't just something that covers the face of the person dancing. The dancer, the choreography, the music swirling through the body: All this is the mask.

Well then, when you finish your work, can I wear it?

This isn't a mask. It's an ntela, *or, if you like, a charm.*

For God's sake, Granddad! Do you really believe that stuff?

It doesn't matter what I think. What matters is what the dead think. Without this—and he turned the piece of wood over in his hands—*without this our ancestors will remain far removed from Kulumani. And you will remain far from the world.*

Forgive me, Granddad: but you, an educated man, should have abandoned these beliefs long ago . . .

He gave me a vague, benign smile: That was his answer. Then he chided me. I shouldn't throw leftovers of food into the garden.

It attracts animals . . .

Maybe that's what I wanted: I wanted to lure the animals to the house, to reinstate the disorder of the jungle, to turn the hen coops into vultures' nests.

In time, these nightly fits got worse: I awoke to torn sheets. Objects lay scattered across the floor of my bedroom.

This is no longer hunger, I'm ill. What's happening to me, Grandfather? I asked, tearful.

The reason for this malady was a secret, Adjiru replied, on one occasion. A secret kept so deep that it had even forgotten about itself.

I don't understand, Grandfather. You're making me scared.

It was true I was ill. But this illness was the only thing protecting me from my past.

The problem isn't yours, dear granddaughter. The problem lies in this house, in this village. Kulumani is no longer a place, it's an illness.

Kulumani and I were sick. And when, sixteen years ago, I had fallen for the hunter, my passion was no more than an entreaty. I was merely asking for help, silently beseeching him to save me from this illness. Just as writing had previously saved me from madness. Books brought me voices like shade in the open desert.

Following Archie's departure all those years ago, I had even thought of writing to him. I would have written endless letters in response to the deep desire I felt. But I never did. No one loved words more than I. But at the same time, I was scared of writing, I was scared of becoming someone else and then, later, no longer being able to return to myself. Just like my grandfather, who surreptitiously carved little pieces of wood, I had a secret occupation. A word drawn on a piece of paper was my mask, my charm, my home cure.

Today, I know how right I was to keep these letters for myself. Archie Bullseye would, indeed, have been suspicious if he had received letters written by me. In Kulumani, many people are surprised by my ability to write. In a place where the majority of folk are illiterate, people find it strange that a woman knows how to write. And they think I learned it at the mission, with the Portuguese priests. But in fact, my schooling dates from before: If I learned to read, it was thanks to the animals. The first stories I heard were about wild animals. Throughout my life, fables taught me to distinguish right from wrong, to unravel the good from the bad. In a word, it was the animals who began to make me human.

This training occurred without a plan, but with a purpose. My grandfather and father would bring home the meat we ate and the furs we sold from their hunting expeditions. But my grandfather brought something extra. From the bush, he would bring little trophies that he gave me: claws, hooves, feathers. He would leave these remnants on a table by the front door. Underneath each of these adornments, Adjiru Kapitamoro would write a letter on an old piece of paper. An *e* for an eagle's feather, a *g* for a goat's hoof, an *m* for *munda*, the word for an arrow in our local language. That was how the alphabet paraded before my eyes. Each letter was a new color through which I looked at the world.

On one occasion, there was a lion's claw reposing on the piece of paper. Crouching next to me, my grandfather rolled his tongue around the roof of his mouth, and, like the sound of a small whip, he emitted a resounding *l*. His hand led mine while I drew the letter on the paper. Afterward, I smiled, triumphant. For the first time in my life, I was coming face-to-face with a lion. And there the beast was, written on the paper, kneeling at my feet.

Careful, my dear granddaughter. Writing is a dangerous form of vanity. It fills the others with fear . . .

In a world of men and hunters, the word was my very first weapon.

I peer at the village square from the top of the guava tree in the garden. I've never seen the *shitala* so full. They've had lunch, they've been drinking, and the sound of their voices has increased. I can't see the guests who are hidden by the porch. I settle myself on the smooth trunk, and breathe in the scent of the guavas to pass the time while I wait. All of a sudden I see Archie emerge into the square to get some fresh air. He hasn't changed much: He's heavier, but still has the same princely air. My heart thumps in my chest. High up in the tree, I have the sensation of being above the world and time.

Suddenly I see Naftalinda crossing the square, sure-footed. What is she doing in a place that's forbidden to women? I've known her ever since she was a young girl, I shared my solitude at the church mission with her. Some people say that her weight has made her mad. I have faith in her insanity. Only small fits of madness can save us from the big one.

The sight of the square full of people draws me back in time. I recall the occasions my grandfather, Adjiru, would come and fetch me to go for a walk in the village. Holding my hand, he would lead me to the *shitala*, the hall of the elders. My very presence there was a heresy that only he could authorize. The elders would ask Adjiru about his hunting adventures. At first he would hesitate. Sometimes he would pull me into the center of the gathering and proclaim:

You're the one who's going to tell stories, Mariamar.

But I'm a young girl, I've never hunted, I'll never go out hunting...

We've all hunted, we've all been hunted, he would argue.

He was playing for time in order to become the center of the world. For later, he would draw himself up like a colossus, devoid of age, and his words would roll proudly around the room. At a certain point, Adjiru would pause, sigh, his eyes seeking out a target, suggesting that this was going to be a long story. He would sit down, sweating profusely. But it wasn't support that he was seeking. It was a throne. Because from then on, Adjiru Kapitamoro would reign. Indeed, he wasn't recalling the hunt: He was hunting again. In the middle of that gathering, at that very moment, before the gaze of his listeners, my grandfather lay in wait for his prey. And in its tense silence, the assembly feared putting to flight not the hunter's memories, but the animals he was chasing.

Tell us another story, Adjiru. Tell us about that time when...

My grandfather would raise his arm in reprimand. He refused the invitation: In a hunter's tale, there's no such thing as "once upon a time." Everything is born right there, as his voice speaks. To tell a story is to cast shadows over the flame. All that the word reveals is, in that very instant, consumed by silence. Only those who pray, surrendering their soul completely, are familiar with the way a word ascends and then plummets into the abyss.

One night, the story had been going on for a long time, and everyone was well oiled with drink, when Genito Mpepe, his voice slurred, interrupted:

Hey, there, Adjiru! You're a hell of an imposter!

It was like a stone thrown into a puddle without any water. Adjiru's astonished look was like a wound ready to be opened. Raising his finger, he declared rancorously:

You, Genito, have just snapped the fork when it's still in the mouth.

Shattered, my grandfather withdrew from the *shitala* and melted into the night. Only I went with him. I sat down in the dark and waited for him to speak. Finally, after a long pause full of sighs, he complained:

Why? Why did Genito do this to me?

My father's drunk.

Ungrateful. Ungrateful, the lot of them. What they call lies, I call gifts.

His gaze became lost in infinity. A thousand thoughts swept through Adjiru, a thousand memories. Gradually, his anger subsided.

Do you know something, Mariamar? The saddest thing is that Genito may be drunk, but he's right. All that bragging in my tales: It's all smoke and no fire.

You shouldn't trust the hunter, he admitted. Not because the hunter is a liar. But because hunting contains the truth of a dance: bodies in flight from their own reality. This was how Adjiru understood it.

In fact, he explained, a hunter's career is made up of fiascoes and forgetfulness. No matter how perfect his aim, a man who hunts is a bungler. For one victory, he has to suffer a thousand defeats. That's why the hunter is an inventor of his own prowess: because he doesn't believe in himself, because he's more fearful of his own weakness than he is of his most ferocious prey.

I'd rather be a liar. For, at heart, I'm nothing. I've never done anything.

Don't say that, Grandfather. You've done so much hunting.

Do you want to know something, dear granddaughter? In hunting, the prey works harder than the predator.

He wasn't complaining. Deep down, his ambition was to be free of all obligations. Happiness, he used to say, consists in not doing anything: *To be happy is merely to let God happen.* And he fell silent, his hands nervously rubbing his knees.

Suddenly he jumped to his feet, decisive, as if visited by some new spirit. And with firm step, he set off again for the assembly hall. Climbing up on a chair, he puffed out his chest and faced the crowd.

Do you want stories? Well, I'm going to tell you a story. Your story.

Here we go again, some mumbled.

Have you forgotten you were once slaves? Adjiru continued.

We're doomed, others commented.

Or have you forgotten that we were once taken across the ocean? None of us came back. Or have you forgotten about my father, Muarimi Kapitamoro? He was taken to São Tomé, remember?

We're going, the men shouted in chorus. And, turning to me, they added: *Come with us, because the words are going to fall thick and fast now.*

One by one they walked off, until I was the only one left in the hall, my heart in my hands, as I stared at the wobbly chair on top of which my grandfather continued his impassioned rhetoric. I even dared, with timid voice, to call him back into the world.

But at that moment, I was invisible to him. An enraged prophet had taken possession of my old relative.

Do you know why the slaves left no memory? Because they have no grave. One of these days, here in Kulumani, no one will have a grave anymore. And there will no longer be any memory that there were once people here…

Grandfather, let's go home.

Nowadays, we don't even have to be put on ships. São Tomé is right here, in Kulumani. Here, we all live together, the slaves and the slave owners, the poor and the owners of the poor.

At that moment, in the now-empty hall, I watched my grandfather Adjiru as if he were a little boy, more solitary and vulnerable than I was. I walked over to the chair that was his stage, and reached up to touch his hand.

Come, Granddad. Let's go home.

Arm in arm, we walked along the path next to the river.

The Hunter's Diary

THREE

A Long, Unfinished Letter

A man sees the mist; a woman sees the rain.
—A PROVERB FROM KULUMANI

That same night, availing ourselves of the most lavish hospitality they could provide, we are installed in the administration building. It is suggested that we shift the piles of folders belonging to the archive to one side, and that we use one or two threadbare sofas that were rotting away there. That way, we would have some improvised tables and beds.

Exuding bonhomie, the administrator bids us good night as he leaves, and, smiling broadly, says:

Tomorrow a lady from the village will come to do the cleaning and prepare a meal.

It was supposed to be Tandi, our maid, the First Lady corrects him. *But it so happens that she—*

She's indisposed, Florindo cuts in hurriedly.

Indisposed? What do you mean by that, husband? Indisposed?

Makwala pushes his wife gently but firmly out into the front yard. They go on arguing outside. Gradually the sound of their voices fades. They seem to have moved away, but the sound of Naftalinda's nervous footsteps indicates that she is coming back, determined to leave us with the last word:

This is just to clarify things: Indisposed means assaulted, almost killed. And it wasn't the lions that did it. The biggest threat in Kulumani doesn't come from the beasts of the bush. Take care, my friends, take great care.

The woman leaves once more and I think what a miracle it is that there are doors for such girth. I pass my finger along the top of the desk and smile: It's among the dust of time and piles of dead letters that I'm going to write this diary. This manuscript is no more than a long, unfinished letter to Luzilia.

I awaken the writer with unnecessary energy. The man had fallen asleep a short time ago, and he must now be emerging from a deep well.

I need your help. Follow me in the car and with the headlamps on so that I can see in front of me . . .

What's happening?

These guys have filled the paths with traps.

So what?

I'm a hunter, I don't use traps.

I go ahead on foot, while the sleepy writer drives the vehicle slowly behind me. Here and there I pick up traps, which I chuck in the back of the jeep. Farther on I come face-to-face with a structure made of trunks the height of a man, on top of which there's a thatch roof.

It looks like a house, the writer warns.

It's an utegu, *a trap for catching lions.*

I throw a rope around the trunks and tie it to the jeep, ordering Gustavo to reverse and drag the roof and palisade away.

Go on, harder, put your foot down!

The straining of the engine, along with my impatient cries, makes me recall my childhood. I remember one time when my father decided I would go with him into the bush. My dear mother opposed this vigorously: Apart from the dangers of hunting, we were in the middle of a war. They argued at the front door to our house, it was early morning and my mother's yells attracted the attention of our neighbors. Old Bullseye decided to put an end to the dispute: He bundled me into the jeep and locked himself in with me. The vehicle reversed in such crazy haste that I was suddenly hurled violently against the windshield, which shattered. The blood flowed hotly down my face. I remember how my mother carried me away, weeping silently. As she lay me on my bed, my blood staining her arms, she declared, mysterious and serene:

Let us be clear about this, husband: This child will never be a hunter.

Once the traps have been collected, I return home, and by the light of an oil lamp open my notebook. I look distractedly at my recollections for the day.

Are you left-handed, then? the writer walks over and asks.

Yes. But I'm right-handed when I shoot.

Then, suddenly inspired, I explain that I hold children with my left hand. I can't do that with the hand that kills.

That's strange, Gustavo responds, *In most cultures, it's the left hand that is ill-fated. What tribe did you get such an idea from?*

From my own, the Bullseye tribe. Nowadays, I'm the only one left in the tribe.

And what are you writing, if that's not an indiscretion?

I'm writing this story.

What story?

The story of this hunting expedition. I'm going to publish a book.

Gustavo can't conceal a nervous smile. My disclosure's had the effect of a punch in the stomach. Questions then follow, one after the other: A book? ... And who is going to publish it? ... And what format would I adopt, a novel, reportage? I put a stop to his barrage of doubts and interrogation. As if to placate him, I ask:

Do you think I won't manage to do it?

And why wouldn't you be able to?

Writing isn't like hunting. You need a lot more courage. Opening yourself up like that, exposing myself without a weapon, defenseless ...

Gustavo understands the irony of my words. Then he decides to attack me on my own terrain:

I've already told you I hate hunting.

So why are you here?

In this instance, there's no alternative if we want to protect human life.

Do you know what I think it is? Fear.

What do you mean?

You're scared.

Me?

You're scared of yourself. You're scared of being hunted by the animal that dwells inside you.

Gustavo turns his back, but I don't give up: No matter how long he might live in a modern, urban world, the primitive bush would still remain alive within him. Part of his soul would always be untamed, full of insuperable monsters.

Come with me to the bush and you'll see: You're a savage, my dear writer.

Call me what you like, but I don't find it at all heroic to fire on defenseless animals. There's no glory in such an unequal contest.

Without a word, I take a lion's claw and tooth from my haversack and place it on the table.

What do you think this is?

They're parts of a lion.

Parts? They're weapons. These are the lion's shotguns. As you can see, the creature is better equipped than I am. So, who's the hunter? Me or him?

This conversation isn't getting us anywhere.

Let me tell you this: For a reporter, you got off to a really bad start.

Why's that?

You didn't understand why I destroyed the traps.

And you got off to an even worse start: Before destroying them, you didn't even bother to speak to the people who'd spent so much time making them.

Do you know something, my writer friend? It would be better if I'd come here to hunt vampires rather than lions. Vampires sell well, and you'd have a guaranteed bestseller.

I blow on the candle and darkness falls over the room. Outside, the full moon awakens some feline restlessness within me. Beneath my closed eyelids, my mind returns again to Luzilia. Suddenly, however, another vision emerges before me. It's a beautiful young black girl. It's a local girl smiling on the riverbank. She is faceless, and could be any woman from the village. Tonight, I sleep with all the women of Kulumani.

I hadn't been asleep for long before I heard roars. The world re-mained in suspense. A lion's growl leaves no silence in its wake.

Can you hear? the writer asked, in a panic.

It's a lioness. It's still a long way off.

The roars gradually faded away. Silence fell over the dark-ness. At last, I could begin my war with the night.

Ever since early morning, a woman called Hanifa Assulua has been sweeping, washing, cleaning, heating up water, without uttering a single word. Her presence has the discretion of a shadow. Only when she leaves does she address me, but without looking up.

Do you remember me? she asks.

I have no recollection. I explain the fleeting nature of my visit. So much time had passed since I had come here to hunt a crocodile. It had just been a few days and then I'd left and never come back again. I'm trying to excuse myself for any eventual indelicacy. But she seems relieved at my lack of memory.

Tell me the truth: Have you just come here to hunt? Or have you come to take someone away from Kulumani?

Who? I don't know anyone.

That's good. It's not as if there was anyone here.

And she said nothing more to me then or on the following days. She did her rounds devoid of body, of voice, or of presence. As far as the writer was concerned, the woman was our conduit to the village community. And there was more to it than that: She was the mother of the latest victim of the lions. That's why Gustavo follows the maid's every step like a shadow. Hanifa is filling a can of water when the writer asks her about the circumstances surrounding her daughter's death.

What happened that night? Was she out at that time of night?

The lion was inside.

Inside the house?

Inside, she repeats, almost inaudibly.

She points at her chest as if to suggest a further meaning to the concept of insideness. Then she raises the can in her arms, refusing any help to place it on her head.

I have to go home. I still have to cook, to prepare your welcome banquet.

She draws herself up, proud and erect, as if the can of water were part of her body, as if it were the water that was carrying her along.

The administrator appears midmorning to introduce the tracker who will accompany us on our hunting expeditions. His name is Genito Mpepe, and he's the husband of Hanifa, the woman who cleans our house. That's how Florindo introduces him. Then, in veiled tones, he adds:

The girl who was killed . . . was this man's daughter . . .

I roll out a map on the table and ask the man to show us where the victims were attacked.

I can only read the land. Maps are a language I don't know.

That's how the tracker answers me. His ways are abrupt, almost rough. I know this type of person. Uncouth in speech, but excellent in the art of hunting. But something makes me think Genito harbors some resentment, some offense toward me.

Am I going to have a right to a weapon?

No. I reply in the same terse terms. The administrator tries to break the ice by exclaiming with exaggerated enthusiasm:

Our hunter has an explanation for the lions' attacks. Explain this to Comrade Genito, he needs to know...

As far as I was concerned, it was obvious: The country folk had exterminated the smaller animals, the food supply for the larger carnivores. In despair, these had started to attack the villages. People are easy prey for the lions. This rupture in the food chain—I used this precise term with some petulance—was the reason for the lions' unusual behavior.

Pigs, the tracker says accusingly, turning toward us.

At first I think he is insulting us.

It's the pigs' fault! he repeats.

The writer looks up to express his incomprehension. But then he gives up: Incomprehension has been his most notable activity since arriving in Kulumani. At that point, Genito Mpepe concludes:

It was the pigs that showed the lions how to get here.

The wild pigs would visit the kitchen gardens, attracted by the crops planted around the houses. The lions followed on their trail and so broke into a space they'd never dared invade before.

Later, while tidying my things, I catch the writer taking a look at my diary. I don't interfere. I let his greedy fingers turn the pages of my little notebook. In fact, rather than finding it irritating, I'm filled with an unexpected vanity at his interest. Could it be that the artist himself recognizes the value of my artistic endeavors?

I don't know—I'll never know—what Gustavo thinks of what he is reading. What I do know is that at a certain point, his hands tremble and there's a glint in his eye.

———

The sight of the papers shaking in Gustavo's hands takes me back to my childhood. Once again, I see the day when Roland was obliged to check the true content of the missives that my mother spent her time composing. And my father, arms crossed on his chest, awaiting the supreme judgment. Indeed, I also asked myself: Were the letters that Martina wrote faithful to what my father dictated?

This is what happened on that occasion: My father stopped his dictation and stood there in silence for some time.

Well, then? his wife asked, seeing him absorbed.

I don't believe you're writing down what I told you to, he replied, advancing resolutely toward his wife.

Henry Bullseye brusquely snatched the letter from his wife's hands. He turned the sheet over, this way and that, next to his face as if he were looking through the paper. For me, this was proof of what I had long suspected: My father couldn't read.

Roland, my son, come here.

My brother got up, quivering from his soul to his feet. Our old man handed him the notebook, staring fixedly at his firstborn.

Read out loud what's written here.

Roland stared wide-eyed as if struggling to focus clearly. The lines danced before his trembling hands. His voice was all of a muddle, unsure of where to begin.

Read!

Where, Father?

Read. Read wherever you like.

My mother looked at him imploringly. Roland stared at me aghast, terrified. Then he took a deep breath, and I didn't even recognize his voice as it rang through the room:

My darling Henry, my beloved husband . . .

Go on, continue…

… One and only love of my life.

I examined my mother's face and I saw her sadness, the sadness of all humanity.

It isn't long before the welcoming banquet, scheduled to take place in the center of the village, is going to begin. The writer wants to gain time and make use of the hour before it starts to interview witnesses and take down statements. I go with him. We wander haphazardly along the paths of Kulumani. I walk in front, my rifle over my shoulder, my gait military. The writer asks me why I need a weapon in the middle of the day, and in the middle of the village.

Animals have a different way of distinguishing between night and day, bush and village.

I begin to get an idea of the size of the village. The huts extend over the other side of the river and cover the slopes on the opposite bank. The village has grown since the last time I was here. Those who have settled along the banks of the Lideia are almost certainly war refugees.

The villagers greet us, standing aside to let us pass along the narrow paths. Some seem to remember me. And I go along distributing pleasantries:

Umumi?

Nimumi, they answer merrily, astonished to hear me greet them in the local language.

They smile. But their happiness gives way to a look of apprehension. These men are bound together by the same vulnerability: They are doomed, awaiting the final blow. For centuries they have existed in the margins of the world. That's why they are suspicious of this sudden interest in their suffering. This suspicion explains the reaction of one of the countrymen when Gustavo asks to interview him:

Do you want to know how we die? No one ever comes here to find out how we live.

Mangy dogs cross our path like wandering shadows. Yet these dogs, at first so shy, surrender to the slightest caress and nestle against our hands as if they yearned to be people. The writer calls them, and tries to stroke them. People watch him, puzzled: They don't expect dogs to be caressed, much less spoken to. These domestic creatures are never addressed by word, nor are they given any scraps of food: They just eat what they can hunt, so that they won't begin to take existence for granted.

Dozens of villagers have gathered together under the mango tree out of curiosity. It's incredible how someplace so deserted can suddenly fill up with folk who seem to have emerged from the sand. I look at this trading of self-interest with cynicism. The writer is a bird of prey: He seeks tales about the war. The villagers expect some gratification. A gift, in local parlance. How can someone criticize me for my professional activity? I practice hunting. Well, the writer lives on carrion. He embarked on this journey in order to peck at misfortune, among survivors who sorrow in silence.

Scratching at the wounds of the past: That's what Gustavo is doing by dragging up memories of the civil war.

What do you remember most about the war?

There's nothing to remember, my good sir, one of the countrymen replies.

What do you mean by that?

We all came back from the war, dead.

I turn my face away. I don't want anyone to detect the vengefulness in my smile. No war can be recounted. Where there's blood, there are no words. The writer is asking the dead to show him their scars.

It's then that I realize what the pleasure is that I get out of hunting: to delve back beyond life, free from being a person.

The blind man who followed us around the night we arrived is in the crowd waiting to be interviewed. At one point, he leans on the shoulders of the person in front of him and salutes us extravagantly. He is still barefoot, wearing the same military fatigues.

Which army did you fight for? the writer asks.

I fought in all of them, comes the immediate reply. And pointing toward me, he adds: *And I remember that gentleman's voice very well.*

My voice? That's impossible.

Forgive me, I don't want to offend, but I'd like to ask you a question: Why did they send for a hunter? They should have summoned me, a soldier.

I don't understand, the writer argues. *What's this got to do with soldiers?*

Don't you see? This, my good sir, isn't a hunt. This is a war.

It was war that explained the tragedy of Kulumani. Those lions weren't emerging from the bush. They were born out of the last armed conflict. The same upheaval of all wars was now being repeated: People had become animals, and animals had become people. During battle, bodies had been left in the bush, along the roads. The lions had eaten them. At that precise point, the creatures of the wild had broken a taboo: They had begun to see people as prey. At last, the blind man brought his long speech to a close:

We men are no longer in charge. Now it's they who control our fear.

Then he pontificated eloquently and without interruption:

The same thing happened in colonial times. The lions remind me of the soldiers in the Portuguese army. These Portuguese took over our imagination so effectively that they became powerful. The Portuguese weren't strong enough to defeat us. That's why they organized it so that the victims killed themselves. And we blacks learned to hate ourselves.

The old man spoke, full of certainty, as if he were giving a speech. At that moment, he was a soldier. An imaginary uniform enveloped his soul.

The writer knows this: The real interview will happen during the welcoming reception scheduled for the lunch to be held in the *shitala*, the open-sided hall in the center of the village. It's in this patch of shade that the men habitually hold their meetings. Women are excluded. They don't even dare walk past this covered space. Florindo Makwala would rather it were taking place somewhere else, more modern, less subject to the dictates of tradition. But the writer was insistent: Under one roof, he would be able to pit all the various explanations for these feline assaults against one another.

The administrator has not yet arrived when, at last, we enter the hall. He was following the protocols of power: He was the one awaited. The elders get to their feet to welcome us. When they greet me, they do so with their left hand supporting their right elbow. It's an act of respect, a sign of esteem. They are trying to tell me my arm has "weight."

Finally, Florindo Makwala appears, accompanied by his bodyguard and a secretary carrying a briefcase. An elderly rustic gets to his feet with a certain cautious respect, and welcomes the administrator with the following words:

We never see you here, in this shitala. *Welcome to the core of the village. Take a seat, but remember that we are the ones to speak first here . . .*

Very well, the administrator agrees. *Afterward, when we've finished, I'll formally close the session . . .*

The old man waits for Florindo to take his seat and then immediately confronts me and Gustavo, hands on hips:

Why are you visiting us?

Haven't you been told? the writer asks in surprise.

We want to know why we were chosen.

So what's the problem?

The others, from the other villages that haven't been visited, will complain. We'll be victims of their envy, and we, who are already dying, will die even more because of what you've done.

We can't visit everyone, I argue, in support of Gustavo Regalo in his efforts. *Besides, what are you talking about? People are dying, and not a week goes by without another victim.*

Time isn't a running race. The legs of time lie within us. Apart from this, many more people are going to die now. By visiting Kulumani, you're summoning the killer lions.

If you don't want me here, I'll go, I declare, getting up from my chair. *I'll go back to the city right now.*

The administrator raises his arms anxiously, and tells us all to sit down. Then he addresses the assembly in Shimakonde. It's obvious he's trying to correct any misunderstandings that might arise. Silence follows. The flustered old man ends up smiling and addresses us in Portuguese:

It's all right. Let's eat first. Then, when our bellies are full, it will be easier to talk.

They give us a plate of cooked mealie flour that's called *shima* around here. A huge pot in the middle is filled with chunks of goat. There are whole pieces of the animal there: the head, the hooves, the meat, the horns. I stick with the flour and some dribbles of a sauce whose origins I would rather not know.

Don't stand on ceremony, Makwala reassures me. *This is the goat you offered the villagers.*

We are served *lipa* and *ugwalwa*, fermented drinks, and I don't commit the indelicacy of not accepting, although I only wet my lips. Before the meal, a bowl of warm water was passed around for us to wash our hands. In the absence of a cloth, I let the water run down my drooping arms. We eat in silence. Only the sound of feverish chewing can be heard. Only when the bones, sucked free of all meat, are returned to the pot does someone address us. The old man was right: The atmosphere is less tense, there's laughter and jokes are told. Gustavo and I are asked if we have wives. They all exchange glances when we reply in the negative.

Neither of you is married?

Suspicion suddenly reestablishes itself: So manlike and yet single? We could only be witch doctors, for only they remain single their whole lives.

Forgive us for doubting, but do you gentlemen live according to the ideology of God?

The old man launches forth again. He comments on our refusal to serve ourselves from the big pot. Who in this world would turn down such an invitation?

They're deceiving us, brothers. These whites eat meat every day. It's this greed of theirs that will put an end to the world.

The problem, another countryman corrects him, *isn't what they eat but how they eat.*

What do you mean? Gustavo asks.

You eat on your own. Only witch doctors do that.

The man rolls a chunk of *shima* in his hand, dips it lingeringly in the pureed cabbage, and lets it drip before putting it in his mouth.

People who eat alone have something to hide. You can be sure, Mr. Hunter, it's not us that have received you badly. You're the ones who've arrived badly.

Let's put all this aside, the writer proclaims in a conciliatory tone. *What I want to ask is this: Are these lions that have appeared real?*

What do you mean, real? comes a chorus of voices.

They explain their surprise: There's the bush lion, which in these parts is called an *ntumi va kuvapila*; there's the invented lion they call an *ntumi ku lambi-dyanga*; and then there are the lion-people, known as *ntumi va vanu*.

And they're all real, they conclude unanimously.

All of a sudden a woman's voice is heard joining in, unexpected and heretical:

It should be another type of hunt. The enemies of Kulumani are right here, they're in this assembly!

This intervention alarms those present. Surprised, the men turn to face the intruder. It's Naftalinda, the administrator's wife. And she's challenging the most time-honored prohibition: Women should not enter the *shitala*. Much less are they authorized to state an opinion on matters of such gravity. The administrator hastens to put things right:

Comrade First Lady, please, this is a private meeting…

Private? I can't see anything private here. And don't look at me like that, because I'm not scared. I'm like the lions that attack us: I've lost my fear of men.

Naftalinda, please, we're meeting here in accordance with age-old tradition, Makwala pleads.

A woman was raped and almost killed here in this village. And it wasn't the lions that did it. There's no longer anywhere I can't go.

She advances proudly past the elders, smiles disdainfully at the administrator, and eventually stops in front of me:

Have you come back to Kulumani, Archangel Bullseye? Well, then, get hunting these rapists of women.

Mama Naftalinda, you've got to ask to speak, Florindo Makwala warns.

The floor's mine, I don't need to ask anyone. I'm talking to you, Archie Bullseye. Aim your weapon at other targets.

What's all this talk, wife?

You pretend you're worried about the lions that take our lives from us. But I, as a woman, ask you: What life is there left to take from us?

Mama Naftalinda, for the love of God. We've got an agenda for this event.

Do you know why they don't allow women to speak? Because they're already dead. Those people there, the powers that be in the government, those who've got rich, they use us to work in their fields.

Maliqueto, please take the First Lady away. She's disturbing our little workshop here.

A few get rich. The dead work through the night for one or two to get rich.

The meeting turns into a riot. Suddenly no one is speaking Portuguese. The acrimony is happening in another world. A world where the living and the dead need translation in order to understand each other.

'my': Do they have pools?
is he hunting her?
Both

Mariamar's Version

FOUR

The Blind Road

A word that can't be spoken eventually turns into poisoned spittle.

—AFRICAN PROVERB

Today, my mother told me she's working as a maid in the administrator's house, where Archie Bullseye is staying. Every day, she passes my hunter. Perhaps she's doing this on purpose, to humiliate me. Without me even asking her, my mother volunteers:

[*This fellow Archie is sick, the sickness of hunters has taken over his body.*]

If her intention is to hurt me, I feign no interest in my reply. I don't want to know. My nation is no longer just the village, or even my own home: It's this solitary spot. The garden where I'm confined.

I contemplate my legs and think how they are now dispensable. I almost miss the time, a while ago now, when I was paralyzed, as if my lower limbs no longer spoke the same language as the rest of my body. That's what I yearn for today: a language my body doesn't understand and that I can only speak in my dreams.

Our feet are born in our head, our whole body begins in our head, just as the rivers descend from the sky. That's what my beloved grandfather, Adjiru Kapitamoro, used to say, and up to this day I think he was right. My legs went to sleep when my head awoke. One day, when I was twelve years old, I fell to the floor next to the bed like an empty sack. The family crowded around me, and Adjiru pulled at my father's jacket:

Was it you, Genito?

I quickly answered in order to protect my old father. No one was to blame, and there was a likely explanation. I'd just had bad dreams during the night, with visions that I dared not remember. They pulled me to my feet and I collapsed again, devoid of any internal support.

Of all times now, in the middle of all this war, my father lamented. *She's going to be yet another burden.*

Since when was a daughter a burden? Adjiru queried.

In childhood, one's body only has one use: to play. But not in Kulumani. The children in our village asked their legs to help them run away in the face of gunfire, faster than bullets. This was the time when our villages were pounded by artillery. At the end of the day, the ritual was always the same: We would pack up our possessions and hide in the bush. For me, this procedure was a game, a recreation shared with the other children. In a world of explosives and blood, we would invent silent pastimes.

In our nocturnal hiding place I learned to laugh inside me, to shout voicelessly, to dream without dreams. Until the day when my lower half was no longer mine. And I fell to the floor next to the bed.

After I became paralyzed, it was my grandfather Adjiru who, at the end of the day, would come and fetch me and carry me off into the forest in his arms. All the others had already withdrawn, and it was just me left, along with one or two worthless objects spread across the floor. While I waited for my grandfather's secure arms, one certainty gripped me ever more forcefully: I was a thing and I would be buried like an object in the dust of Kulumani.

I, Mariamar Mpepe, was doubly doomed: to have only one place in the world and to harbor only one life. An infertile woman in Kulumani is less than a thing. She merely embodies inexistence. People said it was my mother's fault that I was like that. Hanifa Assulua had been cursed. As a result of pressure from the Catholic priests, her family had barred her from being subjected to the rituals of initiation. My mother was a *namaku*, a girl who had never made the transition to womanhood. She had been baptized in the church, but she had never undergone the ceremony of the *ingoma*, which allows a girl to come of age. Hanifa was condemned to eternal childhood.

only embodies existence ⟶ no purpose

My father was certain: After my limbs weakened, I became an encumbrance. But he was unaware that something more serious than paralysis was happening to me. It's true that my pangs of hunger had grown less acute. On the other hand, I began to suffer from unexpected fits. They happened in late afternoon, before *transforming into an animal instead of a woman.*

Animalistic attitudes

we were taken out to our hiding places in the woods. Only Silência knew what was happening inside our room. According to my sister, during these attacks my behavior became totally different from before: I would crawl along on all fours with the dexterity of a quadruped, I would scratch the walls with my fingernails and roll my eyes ceaselessly. Hunger and thirst made me howl and foam at the mouth. To placate my raving, Silência would place plates of food across the floor and bowls of water. Corralled in a corner of the room, my sister, sobbing with terror, would pray for me to stop licking water and biting plates.

It's a spell, it can only be a spell, she whimpered.

Despairing over the cause of all this, Silência reproduced the foundational myth of our tribe right outside our front door: In our garden, she buried a statue that had been secretly carved by my grandfather. Legend had it that a wooden statue, buried in the sands of the savanna by the first man, had turned into the first woman. This miracle occurred at the beginning of the world, but Silência prayed night after night that the little wooden statue in our garden might receive the breath of life.

The statue would never gain a soul, but every time Silência sensed that an attack was imminent, she would hurriedly dig up our little wooden sentinel and bring it to me. Then I would lull the statue as if it were my daughter, and as I rocked it gently, a mother's peace would grow within me. Afterward, I would crawl along, carrying the figurine that I fancied was my legitimate child in my mouth, like a female cat.

My legs might have been lifeless, but I never became my own prisoner. Every morning, children's voices would erupt into the garden.

Come on up, Mariamar, climb up on us!

The boys would take turns giving me piggyback rides and would carry me away far from home, scrambling around joyfully. Carried on their backs like a baby, I experienced every merry little game there was. Today, I can safely say this: I enjoyed a childhood delegated to me by other children. Hanging from someone's neck, riding on some nameless back, I wasn't even aware when my chest rubbed against a boy's sweat.

If you do that, your breasts will never grow, my sister Silência warned.

In Kulumani, breasts are a signal: Depending on their volume, mothers know when they should subject their daughters to the ritual of initiation. What to me was an innocent game was an insult as far as the village was concerned. Women saw me riding on the backs of boys and would turn their faces away in embarrassment. It's in the piggyback position that godmothers, the so-called *mbwanas*, carry the girls who are going to mutate into women to the ceremony. It was this that the women found unforgivable: I was anticipating and disrupting an occasion that they wished to keep sacred and secluded. As the daughter and granddaughter of people educated in Portuguese, I had no place in a world governed by outmoded rules. My sin became even worse because of the time of crisis in which we lived. The more the war robbed us of our certainties, the more we lacked the security of a past ruled by order and obedience.

One day, some boys went to Palma and stole an unused coffin. They brought it back at night and told me:

We've got a sedan chair for you.

From then on, they began to carry me everywhere inside the

coffin. From my palanquin, I would see people stop to show me a respect that they had never given me before. Happy with this general veneration, I declared:

Mother, I want to live in a coffin forever.

But such deference eventually prevented me from realizing that my vanity was indeed sad: I had to cease existing in order for people to take note of my existence. I should yearn for that other carriage of flesh and blood, which had given me such pleasure before: the backs of the other children. But no. Swaying from side to side up there on my improvised throne, my heart was filled with the vanity of a queen.

Just watch my breasts grow now!

Don't wish for that, sister, don't wish to be a woman, Silência warned.

One morning, I awoke to find the coffin in pieces. It was my grandfather, Adjiru Kapitamoro, who had broken it. The old man had unexpectedly strode across the yard and smashed the wooden box to pieces. I even heard him yelling at my parents:

How can you allow this type of tomfoolery? She's a child, for God's sake . . .

I remember I cried as I looked at the broken planks. When she saw me furiously digging in the sand, Silência thought I was looking for the statuette she had buried in the garden. But the grave had another purpose:

I'm burying my coffin.

All this happened before that unforgettable morning when, wearing my shoes and with my hair tidy, I went out with my grandfather. Nor did he explain the reason fully. Only these mysterious words: *You're going to receive the waters of God.*

I was used to his fancifulness. It was he who, when I was still a young girl, had given me the name that would remain with me: Mariamar.

I'm not just giving you a name, he said. *I'm giving you a ship to navigate between ocean and devotion.*

These were his words on the occasion of my second baptism. And he said more: that I didn't need a ritual to be a woman. The woman I would become was already within me.

Catholism = second baptism is very bad

That morning when Adjiru came to fetch me heralded a day when something important was going to happen. Preparations for going out were completed in a trice: A comb was plowed through my unkempt hair and my feet were squeezed into some improvised footwear.

Have you put your shoes on? my grandfather checked.

Why the need for shoes? For a long time now, they had been a mere ornament for me.

Do my parents know where we're going?

Don't be scared, I'm your principal grandfather.

And he chatted away while he tidied my hair.

Bless yourself, dear granddaughter. You're going to receive a miracle.

What miracle, Grandfather?

You're going to walk again.

Whether it was an illness or a curse, he couldn't remain resigned in the face of my descent into the condition of a wild animal. He took a deep breath before declaring:

We have a proverb that goes like this: "If you can talk, you can sing; if

you can walk, you can dance." Well, you're going to sing, you're going to
dance, my dear granddaughter.

I looked at his arm as if it were the continuation of my own
body. And indeed it was. How could I ever cut my second um-
bilical cord? Oblivious to my thoughts, Adjiru Kapitamoro wheeled
me through the village in a little barrow, with the pride of someone invited to inaugurate the square.

Framed by the church door, the priest, Manuel Amoroso,
stood waiting for us. The Portuguese missionary was the only
white man we knew. We didn't distinguish the man by the color
of his skin or by the language he spoke, or even by his vestments.
What differentiated him from the rest was that he had no wife
that we could discern. Nor children following in his footsteps.

Adjiru Kapitamoro! exclaimed the priest, putting a flourish on
every syllable as if he were chortling a jaunty song.

Indeed, Father.

For the first time, my grandfather's voice sounded fragile to
me, as if it were seeking support. I looked at him against the
light, as if to satisfy myself of his stature. And once again, I took
a breath: Behind his outline, the church tower rose majestically.
That was where our vertical journey to the firmament began. At
that point, getting close to God seemed to me to require the effort of a mountaineer. The church was not inviting me to enter
it, but rather to climb it.

I took time to get used to the brightness once inside. Then I
began to adapt: I'd never seen a house with so much wall. The
same cross hanging on Amoroso's chest dominated, on a much
vaster scale, the center of the building. Upon the wooden cruci-
fix rested this world's second white man: bearded, half naked,
and covered in wounds.

Kneel before Christ, Amoroso ordered.

She can't, Father. Have you forgotten why she's come here to the mission?

Let us help her. She must do it.

The two men suspended me by my arms and then let go. I collapsed like a wet cloth. I lay spread-eagled on the floor and from that angle contemplated Amoroso and Christ. The two white men were alike: sad and wizened, as if life were happening in some other, inaccessible place. Christ displayed his wounds, Amoroso exhibited his bereaved gaze. Both of them summoned me toward the great family of the suffering. Toward the family that, only in suffering, feels close to God.

So have you come to a decision regarding my little girl?

My grandfather was irritated by the use of the possessive. My little girl?

This granddaughter of mine will always be mine, and I'm leaving her here only until she can walk again—these were his angry words as he left the church. *I myself will come and fetch her and take her back to our home when she can stand on her own two feet*, my grandfather promised emphatically.

The Portuguese priest didn't seem to hear. He was totally absorbed in contemplating the church ceiling as if he were look-ing beyond what he was actually seeing. He stood there motion-less, unaware that Adjiru had already left. He was satisfied: In a predominantly Muslim region, the representation of a miracle could bring in believers and approval. Smiling, he told me:

When your dear old granddaddy dies, he'll go straight to heaven.

My grandfather will never die!

As far as I was concerned, Adjiru Kapitamoro's life was that of a tree: Rooted in the ground, he already belonged to the sky.

My grandfather's visits were the high point of the two years I spent at the mission. On some occasions, he would sit silently, gazing at the horizon. Other times, he wanted to know whether God was paying me any attention.

And how's your writing? he would ask.

I'm always writing, Grandfather. Do you want to read it?

No, my dear. If I read, do you know what will happen? I'll stop seeing the world. Read me the story of the queen of Egypt.

It was his favorite text. I already knew it by heart. Grandfather would close his eyes and I would recite it, always in the same tone:

It is said that Ra, the sun god of ancient Egypt, weary of the sins of men, created the goddess Sekhmet to punish those who needed to be punished. And that's what the goddess did, with an excess of zeal, according to some. Sekhmet's vengefulness even began to fall upon the innocent. In despair, the followers of Ra asked the god to help, but he was unable. So the Egyptians had the idea of creating a drink that was the color of blood, and they managed to inebriate the goddess. As a result, she fell asleep and once again fell under the control of Ra.

When the story was finished, my grandfather remained with his eyes closed. Then, he kissed my hands, saying: *You, my granddaughter, are my goddess.*

Adjiru's constant presence at the mission gave me peace of mind, but threw into relief other absences. One time, I managed to overcome my fear:

Grandfather, tell me something: Are my parents saddened by me?

It's just that the war is now taking up all our time. That's why they don't visit you. Everyone's gone, and I and one or two others of no importance are the only ones left.

Aren't you scared of being killed?

I'm so skinny that any bullet would miss me.

In truth, the sound of gunfire and explosions was increasing in the vicinity. Father Amoroso was called to conduct funerals ever more frequently, and at an ever greater distance. The inhabitants of Kulumani, including my parents, had moved to Palma months ago. Only Adjiru and his five brothers remained. They were convinced that they would be spared because they were elderly. But it wasn't their age that saved them. They paid for their security. What they hunted was given to the soldiers of both armies.

That's how things are, Mariamar, Adjiru recalled. *In war, the poor are killed. In peace, the poor die.*

One time, the Kapitamoro clan brought the eldest of the brothers to the church. His name was Vicente and he was wounded, shedding blood, his weakened feet dragging along the ground. Held up by his brothers' arms, Vicente entered the holy sanctuary, unable to see anything in front of him through the prevailing shadows. He was blind. Yet it was he who showed his brothers the way. He knew the church like the palm of his hand. He had built those walls that now offered him shelter.

They sat him on the long wooden bench, supporting him shoulder to shoulder. Adjiru walked over to the priest and addressed him in a tone that mingled entreaty with threats:

This is the house of God, no one can die here. Do you hear me, Father Amoroso?

Let us pray, my son, let us pray.

The Kapitamoros yelled their prayers, and for sure no one had ever prayed with such aplomb before an altar. The booming voices of those demented brothers were intimidating: The gods had better watch out in case there wasn't a miracle.

At first we could still hear our wounded relative babbling. What he was asking for, however, was the exact opposite of what his brothers wanted: He was praying for his Creator to allow him to depart, tired as he was of suffering. What then happened was proof that God doesn't listen to those who shout loudest. Vicente Kapitamoro breathed his last without anyone noticing, his devoted fingers intertwined, his head slumped over his knees.

This incident proved a blow to Adjiru's faith. From then on, he no longer went to mass. He stopped at the entrance to the church and asked his brothers to go in and pray in his name. Let them pretend they were him, let them borrow his name and his soul, that's what he asked.

We're alike. God won't notice.

Unhappy, Father Amoroso reflected on the situation. He was disappointed by Kapitamoro's attitude. However, he couldn't confront such an eminent figure in the village. He waited for time to bring him inspiration. And time brought peace. Gradually Kulumani resumed the life it seemed to have lost forever. The wounds of history healed, and broken affiliations were reforged. The missionary thought it would be good to make use of the wave of reconciliations and requested Adjiru to meet him in the churchyard so as to remind him of his sacred duties.

Tomorrow I shall say a mass for your brother Vicente's soul.

My dear sir, with all due respect, I shall not go.

And why won't you come?

I'll go to the matanga, *our own ceremony for the dead.*

And how will you explain yourself before God?

I'll explain myself before Nungu, our God. With all due respect.

For years he had been criticized for frequenting the mission and converting to Catholicism, and, in the words of Kulumani folk, for having become a *vamissau*. In his own defense, he had argued: *The others have the drum dance, I have the Bible.* In the beginning, Adjiru still had a reason for his apparent conversion: to entrust the drums to the hands of God, and make the sacred book dance. That was why he taught me the art of dancing. Now, however, any purpose had long been abandoned.

Appealing to divine inspiration, Amoroso picked off a long rosary of arguments. The hand of God, he said, is a sightless guide. What this hand seeks is that we should be the masters of our journey. But journeys last as long as a star. By the time we see them, they have long ceased to exist.

All this is just words. What hand of God sends us on a journey to war, Mr. Amoroso?

Why do you call me Mister? Why don't you address me as Father anymore?

You live shut away in your own world. Look what's happening out there. And you'll see that sometimes the gods die in wars...

How can you dare to say such a thing in the house of God?

I'm the one who built this church. I and my brothers. We started building it when we were still slaves.

He paused, measured his words, and in the end burst out, without any rancor, as if he were among friends:

At the time, we should have thrown the church into the river.

Holy Mother of God!

Standing as tall as he could, his voice trembling with emotion, everything in the priest contrasted with my grandfather's tranquillity:

Do you want to see a miracle, Adjiru? Well, look at your grand-

daughter, and turning to me, he ordered, *Show him, Mariamar, show him...*

I got up and walked toward Adjiru. My legs swayed, but my steps were firm. Grandfather didn't seem surprised.

Mariamar can walk again, I'm very happy. But let me ask you this: Have you taught her to kick, Reverend Father?

Kick? Is that something one teaches a girl?

Of course, Father. Precisely because she's a girl, she ought to learn to punch, bite, kick...

Those aren't the words of a believer. Here, we teach people to love one's nearest and dearest.

It's from one's nearest and dearest that we most need to defend ourselves.

He got up and walked around me, his hands tapping his chest as if it were a drum, and he began to wave his arms. Grandfather knew that we were forbidden to dance by the priest.

Can you still dance, Mariamar? Now, then, show me you still know how to kick up some dust.

Amoroso's watchful gaze didn't allow me to sway my hips. I tried one or two clumsy steps around the room and, without waiting, Grandfather raised his arm to put an end to the performance. In a dry tone, he ordered:

Go and pack your bag, because I'm coming to fetch you tomorrow.

The following day, he returned with a small wheelbarrow. I reminded him that I could walk on my own two feet, but he pointed uncompromisingly at the rough-and-ready vehicle and asked:

Do you know what day it is today, my dear?

Today?

You're sixteen today. You've got a right to be carried.

Seated in my little carriage, I crossed the village, listening to the missionary's frantic cries behind me:

Mariamar can walk, it's God's miracle, it's a miracle! She's being wheeled along, but she can walk perfectly. Come and see, for it's a miracle!

I gazed around me, astonished. I hadn't been outside the mission for months. Kulumani was unrecognizable. With the end of war, people had returned to the village. My family had also settled back in our old house. And there seemed to be more inhabitants than ever. A crowd of hawkers filled the road that led to Palma.

At home, only Silência rejoiced in my return. My mother was sifting rice and looked up unenthusiastically. I was the one who spoke after a long silence:

Grandfather says it's my birthday today.

Grandfather invents calendars. That's why he hasn't died yet.

Whatever the day, it's good to be back. To be back now that we've got peace . . .

Without averting her gaze from her sifting, Hanifa Assulua mumbled in an undertone. I was talking of peace? What peace?

Maybe for them, the men, she said. *Because we women still wake up every morning to a timeworn, endless war.*

Hanifa Assulua was in no doubt as to the condition of women in Kulumani. We awoke in the early morning like sleep-deprived soldiers and we got through the day as if life were our enemy. We would come home at night without anyone to comfort us over the battles that we had to face. Mother recited this litany of complaints in one breath, as if it were something she had been waiting a long time to say.

That's why you should have left all this talk about peace back at the mission, dear daughter. During the time you lived there, we had to survive here.

She was accusing me. As if I were the one to blame for her solitude and the unhappiness of all the women. I retreated down the hall with the small steps of a prisoner returning to her cell.

The Hunter's Diary

FOUR

Rituals and Ambushes

[Where men can be gods, animals can be men.]
—THE WRITER'S NOTEBOOKS

Hanifa comes to call me in the middle of the night. She is so terrified that I rush off after her without changing clothes. With a long nightgown hiding my knees, I look like a clumsy ghost.

The lions have reached my house.

They'd been prowling around the village ever since nightfall. Hanifa had heard them in the distance.

I didn't hear anything, I confess.

The woman has no doubts. There are three of them and they're making for the village. We wouldn't hear them again. The closer they get, the more careful they become. I pick up my gun and step out into the garden, gauging the darkness and the silence. Hanifa follows me. The writer, gripped by terror, brings up the rear. In no time at all, we are standing in the Mpepes' yard.

Don't switch on your flashlight, sir, the woman whispers to the writer.

So how am I going to see where I'm going? Gustavo asks.

Be quiet, the pair of you! And you, Hanifa, go and get Genito immediately! I order.

He's sleeping.

Suddenly Hanifa points at some bushes which are stirring and urges me:

Fire, it's the lions! Fire!

My forefinger on the trigger grows taut. In the arch of bone and nerve lies the decision of the gods: whether or not to extinguish a life in a bolt of lightning. But in this case, my quivering finger hesitates. It's a lucky delay: A figure emerges from the shadows, hands raised like a drunken scarecrow.

Don't shoot, it's me, Genito!

The tracker had gone to buy some liquor in the nearby village. He raises the bottle as proof.

Now go inside, Hanifa. You know I don't want you out here at night.

Your wife went to call us, the writer explains, *because she seemed to think there were lions in the neighborhood.*

The tracker looks at the bush from which he has just emerged. He shakes his head, raises the bottle to his lips, and takes a generous swig. He makes sure his wife has gone back into the house. He sits down on the ground and invites us to drink with him. Neither of us accepts. We stand there looking at the stars until Genito breaks the silence.

Hanifa knew it was me. She knew I was on my way home.

I don't understand, says Gustavo.

Do you know what happened here? It was an ambush. Hanifa wants to kill me.

Don't be so absurd...

She thinks I'm guilty of terrible things.

What things?

Our things. You know something? There's no law here, no government, and even God only visits us occasionally.

man considered lion ——▷
Fo he is just as violent (rope)

When I get back to my room, I remove the cartridges from the chamber of my rifle and repeatedly press the trigger. I'm still trembling slightly, but in general my body obeys me immediately. As always, I take time to reconcile myself to sleep. Staring fixedly at the ceiling, I once again picture my last visit to the psychiatric hospital. I can't get Roland's farewell out of my mind—his long hands gain wings and flutter blindly around the room. I spend some time like this. As they say in Kulumani, night only ends when the owls fall silent. Without the presence of these birds, night loses its ceiling. And there are those who, without even being aware, scare these birds of omen away. We have these owl chasers to thank for every new break of day. There at the other end of this remoteness, Roland's hands shape each of my sleepless nights.

First thing in the morning, the administrator bursts hurriedly and furtively into our living quarters as if he were being chased by lions. He glances at the street before shutting the door, wipes his forehead with a handkerchief, and then collapses on the black imitation leather sofa.

My wife mustn't see me here. She's becoming impossible, that woman!

The man is quick to explain himself. He feared we might have got a false impression of what had come out of the meeting in the *shitala*. What had been evident from the meeting was envy. The cancer of our society, as he put it. It was precisely this cancer that had led to the recent dismissal of one of his aides in the administration. The career of a veteran official of the party, one Simon Mutapa, had been summarily destroyed.

Don't you want to put the ventilation on? I've got the generator connected up, and the company delivered more fuel ...

He points over in our direction at a noisy fan. We stand there for some time glancing at each other, waiting for the administrator to catch his breath. Then, once again, he sets off talking, and explains that, prior to our arrival, the people had invented guilty parties for tragic occurrences.

They blamed Simon Mutapa for this curse of the lions.

Rumors were spread around the village that the Mutapa family had invisible powers. It was in Simon's house that lions were made. Logical explanation had been of little use, just as a commission of inquiry sent by the provincial administration had been of little use. Mutapa opened up his house and his private life in order to prove his innocence. They had searched his home, his garden, his work place. They hadn't found any *mintela*, any material that might have been used to create a lion. But they were adamant that he was the fabricator of lions.

So what do these mintela *consist of?* the writer wants to know.

In the old days, *mintela* were merely roots, the bark of trees, bones. Nowadays magic artifacts include the waste products of modern urban life: acid from car batteries, old cell phone casings, computer keyboards.

There must have been a reason for so much suspicion, Gustavo insists.

There was only one basis for their suspicion: The Mutapas had accumulated wealth. For any one of us, the assets of that particular official were sparse, almost invisible. A few acres of sugarcane, one or two banana trees, and a still, where his daughters produced *lipa*. But for the villagers, his affluence was vast and without explanation. In a place where no one can be anything, Simon Mutapa ended up getting noticed. His neighbors were outraged. And neighbors are like medicine: They're very good, but only turn up when there's an illness. Accused of "making" lions, Simon was beaten and threatened with death. The following day, he and his family hit the road and disappeared.

Naftalinda Makwala visits us at the end of the day to warn us that something is being prepared in the village. We should be watchful, and we shouldn't leave the house or expose ourselves. We should keep an eye open without being seen.

If you go out, you risk death!

What's happening? the writer asks anxiously, lifting the corner of the curtain in the window.

Senhor Gustavo? Come away from there! You mustn't look!

The First Lady calls me over to a corner and places herself in front of me, pressing her generous buttocks against my body. From that window, we could look out over the square in front of us.

The men are arriving. Stand here, right by me, she says.

The ritual that precedes a collective hunt, the *kuyola liu*, is about to begin. The square is getting ready to receive the two dozen men who will set out on the hunt for lions in the early hours of the morning. How I wished I could be there to take part in the ritual! Naftalinda understands my disappointment:

You are like me, a woman: We're excluded. Let's keep each other company. Isn't it nice here, in this little patch of shadow?

Shadow? The inside of the house is shrouded in darkness. Outside, the last vestiges of the day are being extinguished. The ritual has been summoned as an emergency. The heads of families, the sons of the soil, want to be the ones to chase away the threat that hangs over the village. They don't want to concede to me, a stranger, the honor of conducting this battle against such powerful, invisible forces.

The menfolk of Kulumani have come together, along with a few others from neighboring villages. Each one is carrying a bow, a shotgun, a cutlass, or a net. They've brought with them food and water, carried in bottles and haversacks. They gather in the open space around the *shitala* and there doesn't seem to be any set agenda for the event, no hierarchy among them. They shoo away the dogs that are beginning to get excited with all the activity. A young boy tries to join the group, but is quickly turned away. He hasn't undergone the rituals of initiation. Gradually, as if in response to some hidden master of ceremonies, chants begin to be heard, and the first timid dance steps are tried. Naftalinda can't resist joining in and her buttocks begin to sway, pressing ever more tightly against me. My head spins and I'm almost thrown off balance. What if the administrator were to catch me in this sultry dance with his wife? Suddenly one of the dancers exclaims:

Tuke kulumba!

It's the call for action. Then, as if carried forward by some invisible wave, the men stamp their feet rhythmically on the ground, and a cloud of dust envelops their bodies.

Now they've kicked up the dust! the First Lady whispers, her face next to mine.

Now, she says, *all I feel is anger, I can't watch any more of this.* And she retreats to the back of the house, joining Hanifa, who is preparing a meal.

Suddenly Makwala the administrator crosses the square. He is accompanied by the policeman. He shouts as he stirs up the dust:

What's going on here? Is this a demonstration? Did you get the necessary authorization?

I take advantage of the First Lady's absence and furtively escape from the house, disobeying the strict instructions to keep myself hidden and shut away. The writer follows me, his camera slung over his shoulder. We join Florindo Makwala in the middle of the square. The villagers stop their ceremony and observe us silently, full of hostility. It's clear by the way they look at us: We are intruders, we are desecrating the occasion. The writer immediately realizes that taking photographs is out of the question. And one word in Shimakonde is enough to bring the administrator to heel, rendering him unable to ask any further questions.

One of the hunters leaves the group and comes over to me to take a bullet from the cartridge belt that I wear across my chest. He examines the projectile, turning it over in his fingers. Then he asks:

Do you know who made it?

Who made the bullet?

Yes.

It's impossible to know . . .

The man smiles arrogantly. Then he raises his spear to the level of his face and, looking straight into my eyes, proclaims:

I know who made my weapon.

Then he dances away from us in a series of acrobatic pirouettes, at each turn touching the ground with the tips of his fingers. He picks up a stone the size of a fist and raises it above his head, this time laying down a challenge to the administrator Makwala. He addresses him in Shimakonde, while the policeman translates for me:

You can sell all of this, the sky, the earth, the waters. You can sell us. But the spirits don't talk to money.

After a few more leaps, the hunter continues his speech:

Of all the stones in the world, there is one that is not of this earth. That is the flying stone.

With all his strength, he hurls the stone into the air with such impetus that it disappears from sight over the canopy of the trees. Everyone knows that the stone will never fall to earth. Turned into a bird, the stone will guide the villagers in their search for their prey. After a pause, the dancing starts again. The policeman warns us:

I don't know whether it's worth our staying here . . .

The men start taking off their clothes. Then they douse their naked bodies with an infusion made from the barks of trees. This mixture will make them immune to any disaster.

I take a look at the rear of the house. Hanifa, her back turned, is busy putting out the kitchen fire. No fire can be lit while this ritual bathing is occurring. Only after the men have finished their washing can Hanifa and all the other women light their fires once again.

The men dance for a little longer, and while they are gyrating and jumping they begin to lose their inhibitions, and soon they are screaming, growling, and soiling their chins with froth and spittle. It's then that I understand: Those hunters are no longer humans. They are lions. Those men are the very animals they seek to hunt. What's happening in the square merely confirms this: Hunting is witchcraft, the last piece of witchcraft to be permitted by law.

Finally, the men leave in silence, and like this, marching in military formation without saying a word, they will search the bush for days on end, without food, drink, or shelter. A strange peace descends upon Kulumani. One by one, the cooking fires are lit again in the huts.

The writer comments ecstatically:

What an unforgettable sight! A performance rooted in Nature. What a pity I couldn't take photographs of it!

Did you like it? Naftalinda asks. She wears an enigmatic, almost defeated smile. But then she asks: *How many men were there in the ceremony?*

About twenty, maybe.

There were twelve in the other group.

The other group? What group?

The ones that killed Tandi, my maid. There were twelve of them. Some of them were dancing here right in front of you.

They killed her?

They killed her spirit, only her body was left. A wounded body, the ruins of a person.

She recounts what had happened: Her maid had inadvertently crossed the *mvera*, the camp accommodating the boys undergoing their initiation. The place is sacred and women are expressly forbidden to enter the area. Tandi disobeyed and was punished: She was raped by all the men. All of them took their turn with her. The girl was taken to the local health center, but the nurse refused to treat her. He was afraid of retaliation. The district authorities received a complaint, but didn't do anything. Who has the courage in Kulumani to rise up against tradition?

My husband remained silent. Even when I threatened him, he didn't do anything . . .

I don't know what to answer. Dona Naftalinda gets up and gazes at the path down which the hunters have disappeared. While still stoking the fire, she murmurs:

I don't know what they're looking for in the bush. The lion is right here in the village.

After night has fallen, the administrator drops by our house. He is agitated, something in the ceremony of the hunters has left him scared. He wants us to organize ourselves for an expedition immediately. He urges us to seize the initiative and kill the lions ourselves.

We can't have these traditionalists getting the better of us.

Florindo Makwala expects some sort of declaration from me, a commitment to act quickly. But I only make a decision after he has left. Under the flickering light of an oil lamp, I inspect my equipment while, at my request, the writer takes responsibility for the vehicle, the fuel, and the flashlights. My instructions to Gustavo are delivered tersely, in an almost military tone. When we go to bed, I explain myself as if to compensate for the authoritarian way my orders were given:

We've got to resolve this quickly. I don't like the atmosphere that's being produced.

Early the next morning, at first light, I drive the vehicle along faintly marked tracks.

Why didn't we bring the tracker? the writer asks fearfully.

Genito has been drinking. Apart from that, I want you to get an idea of the terrain. This is a journey of exploration.

Will we know how to get back? Gustavo asks.

From the backseat, the administrator is in no doubt: We'll get back without any difficulty at all. Even though he's not from Kulumani, he already knows the area. His wife, Naftalinda, accused him of governing while shutting himself away in his office. But it's not true.

I scarcely listen to him, as I'm too busy looking out for animal tracks.

Hanifa was right—the lions have been here.

After a few kilometers we enter one of those clearings that have been opened up to protect the fields where the crops are planted. In the middle of this space there is a leafy tree, and by its bulky trunk we find two half-dressed young boys tied up and with clear signs of having been beaten. We stop and get out of the jeep to find out what happened there.

What's wrong? Florindo Makwala asks in Portuguese.

The boys look at us as if they've been forbidden to speak. The administrator tries to get them to talk, this time in Shimakonde. In vain. They remain silent. Patiently, Florindo insists. They reply by shaking their heads, without ever uttering a word. Makwala tells us what he thinks has happened:

These poor wretches have been accused of being makers of lions. The hunters tied them up when they passed by this way last night. When they return later, they'll carry out their justice.

When we free their wrists, the boys stand there motionless, as if stuck to the trunk of the tree.

You can go, we encourage them.

Where? one of them finally asks.

Wherever you want. You're free now.

They don't move. To me, they seem to have been incorporated into the vegetable matter of the tree. We leave them, while the condemned boys remain rooted to the shadow of their fear. They'll stay there until their executioners return.

I start driving again along paths that are covered in elephant grass. I seem to be traveling in a boat, among green waves rippling away as far as the horizon. The jeep is advancing so slowly that walking would be faster.

At the top of a hill, I stop the vehicle, take off my hat, and pretend to search the sky.

Are we lost? Gustavo asks anxiously.

It's good to be lost. It means there are possible routes. Things get serious when you run out of routes.

I'm asking whether you are still able to find any routes.

Out here in the bush, it's the routes that come and find us.

I hear Florindo Makwala's laugh behind me. The writer's face bears a semblance of humiliation. All my words, all my silence have the effect of an accusation: He is from the city; he can't even come to terms with the ground he treads. The truth of the matter is this: Here in this world, Gustavo needs me as his teacher even to walk along on his own two feet.

When we get back to the jeep, the sun is at its height and the heat causes mirages in the long grass.

I could do with a whiskey on the rocks, Florindo jokes.

The two of them swap rude jokes. All of a sudden I order them to keep quiet. I pretend to be listening carefully to something that has escaped their notice. My solemn tone gives them a fright:

Be quiet, don't leave the car. Under any circumstances, do you hear?

Crouching low, my gun at the ready, I pretend to choose the quietest path and gradually disappear among the bushes. After that, silence reigns, a terrifying solitude surrounds those who wait in the car, frozen with fear. I hear them muttering to each other.

How long is he going to take? Florindo asks.

Their mumbled conversation, which only serves to keep their apprehension at bay, is suddenly interrupted as I decide to fire into the air. To produce even greater fear, I burst headlong out of the undergrowth, leaping over shrubs and yelling for us to get out of there. The writer jumps behind the wheel and the jeep lurches forward at startling speed.

What's happened, Archie? the writer asks, tremulous.

I can't tell you.

The administrator remains silent. If I can't recount the cause of my terror, then what has happened escapes human reason. When we arrive back in the village, I retire without saying a word. From my room, I hear Florindo and Gustavo talking:

What in heaven's name happened?

How would I know?

I'm beginning to suffer the same beliefs as these wretched folk. Who knows, maybe he saw one of those things . . .

One of those things . . . ?

Yes, the lame serpent, for example.

The administrator explains himself: In the village there's a serpent that moves around over the silence of ceilings and over distant paths. This venomous creature seeks out happy people in order to bite and poison them, without their ever being aware. This is why, in Kulumani, everyone suffers from the same unhappiness. Everyone is scared, scared of life, scared of love, even scared of their friends. Some folk call this monster a "devil." Others call it a *shetani*. But most call it the "lame serpent." The writer interrupts this long narrative:

Forgive me, my dear administrator, but as far as I am concerned, this serpent is ourselves.

Mariamar's Version

FIVE

Some Honey Eyes

It is easier to hear a pretty girl's murmur than a lion's roar.

—ARAB PROVERB

It was my honey eyes that captivated Archie Bullseye when he visited us for the first time sixteen years ago. The hunter found me on the side of the road and, without knowing it, saved me from the forays of Maliqueto Próprio, the policeman. I've already talked about this. But I didn't mention that Archie had returned some days later to make overtures and promises. He said he wanted to take me away to the city. And that we would be happy and forget about all that we had gone through before.

Come with me, the hunter insisted. *Let's find happiness together.*

Terrified, I refused. What he was promising was far beyond

what I could ever dream. I looked around me to see whether someone was listening to us. We were talking in the kitchen yard, that little space where women most forget about what it is to live. I looked at the stove that was forever lit, the firewood piled up, the saucepans laid out facedown. I examined all this as if it were the work of no one at all. As if the embers were not gathered up from our kitchen to light a neighbor's fire. As if women's hands were not ensuring that the fire never went out.

Have you nothing to say, Mariamar?

To listen is also to talk. The hunter was talking about things I didn't know: the city, happiness, love. How good it was to hear his talk, how bad for me it was to hear his words! But I didn't succumb to his invitations. In the end, happiness and love are similar. You don't try to be happy, you don't decide to fall in love. You're happy, you love.

We'll be happy, Mariamar.

Who told you I want to be happy?

He contemplated me as if I were speaking a language he didn't understand.

That night, the drums beat and there was dancing. At first I stood motionless, watching the others shake their bodies sensuously, while the ground shook as if the drums were beating in the depths of the earth. I managed to hold myself back until my feet were ignited. To free myself from this fire, I surrendered gradually to the rhythm of the music, gyrating across the moonlit yard. Seeing me dance, Archie came over and put his arm around my waist, inviting me to turn with him.

Let go of me, huntsman, dancers don't touch each other here.

I don't care, I dance the way I know.

I remembered what the men of Kulumani said: No one hunts with anyone else. Well, dancing is like hunting. Each dancer takes possession of the whole world. I spun around before facing him:

I'm not dancing with you. I'm dancing for you. Go and sit down and watch me become a queen.

He obeyed submissively. As for my performance, it stopped obeying me. For I found myself dancing naked across the yard, rolling on the ground, little by little losing my human composure. Archie collapsed in surrender, speechless and without gesture. Seeing him like that, weak and defenseless, made me feel even more womanly. I whispered sweet nothings in his ear and he melted away in my embrace. We didn't even notice that the fire had gone out: Another fire had been lit within us.

While I was getting dressed, I told Archie what he was waiting for so hopefully:

Early tomorrow morning, come and get me. I'm going to run away with you.

I certainly shall. Before the village wakes up, I'll pass by here and fetch you.

That night, I was visited by all possible dreams. Until morning broke, I remained by my bedroom door, my hands clutching the case that lay in my lap. My future was packed away in that case. Folded away neatly like clothes, my hopes and dreams lay waiting.

I never got as far as unpacking that case. For, the following morning, the hunter didn't come to get me. Forgetfulness, I thought, to mitigate any doubts. A minor lapse that Archie would put right later on: He would return to Kulumani, and, to prevent any delays, my little suitcase would remain packed.

Little by little, like someone dying without being ill, I submitted to the evidence: Archie had abandoned me. One by one, my dreams turned into a recurrent nightmare: From my dreams, indistinct voices emerged:

Dombe! Dombe!

In the distance, beyond the morning mist, people were shouting. They took us for creatures of the white race. That was why they were calling us *dombe*, which is the name given to fish. Ever since the Portuguese arrived here centuries ago, this is the word used to describe them. Washed up on the beaches, coming from the liquid horizon, they could only have been born in the ocean. Which was where we came from, Archie and I.

Lying unconscious by my side, the hunter seemed to have given up. That was my nightmare: Archie and I were washed up on a beach as we fled downstream in a dugout. The current had taken us out beyond the estuary and deposited us on the shoreline, among the bits and pieces scattered along the sand.

Gradually, shadows emerged from the dunes, shapes rushed toward us, unrestrained. They're coming to save us, I thought. But when they leaned over us, what they did was rob us of our clothes and possessions. The angry cries of the crowd grew louder and louder, as they rhythmically egged each other on:

Dombe, dombe!

Don't kill us, please don't kill us, I implored them, sobbing.

You're fish, we're going to gut you.

I'm a person! I'm black, look at me!

It was then that I realized how ridiculous my situation was. How can anyone prove their own race? I tried to speak in Shimakonde, but not a single word came to me. Once again, the chanting shouts, like some ritual of execution. Suddenly a vision emerged from the misty background: Genito Mpepe, cutlass in hand, commanding his ululating horde:

Dombe! Dombe!

It was the end. My father prepared to knife my lover. Lying lifeless next to me, Archie had no idea of the immediate danger. As quick as a flash, the cutlass sliced through the air but didn't reach its victim. All of a sudden the hunter's body turned to liquid, wave after wave until it became ocean, nothing more than ocean. Archie was saving himself at the very last moment, transformed into water. In my dream, I too gave in to this final impulse, joining my beloved in his fate. As no one came to my rescue, I chose to melt into another substance.

The dream taught me I had one decision to make: I wanted to die by drowning. I have never wanted anything so much as that. To die in water is to return. That was what I felt the first time I saw the ocean: a yearning for a womb to which I was returning at that moment. A yearning for that gentle death, that beating of a double heart, that water which, after all, is what our whole body is made of.

My mother, Hanifa Assulua, used to complain that in Kulumani we were all buried. It was the opposite. We were drowned, that's what it was. All of us had been drowned before we were even born. At our birth, we were delivered onto the first beach we washed up on.

Tonight my father knocked on my bedroom door. Curious, I opened the door slightly:

I'm going into the bush with the visitors. Tomorrow we're going to hunt lions.

Never before had my father come to say goodbye. He would leave in the early morning, and no one would notice him going. But this time, he looked at me with lifeless eyes, and touched my neck as he used to when I was a little girl.

Don't touch me! I reacted violently.

I just came to say goodbye, he mumbled submissively.

I was astonished to have merited this farewell. In Kulumani, fathers don't pay any attention to their daughters, rarely speak to them, and never show any sign of affection toward them, much less in public. Affection is a mother's task. Why, then, was Genito Mpepe giving me this sudden and unexpected display of attention? Then it occurred to me: He wasn't just taking his leave. He was saying sorry. Genito Mpepe knew that he wouldn't return from the expedition. So he had come to ask for forgiveness. He was asking my forgiveness for never having been my father. Or what was worse still: for only having been my father in order not to let me be a free, happy person.

It's strange how much our heart rules our head. For years, I had wished for and imagined his end. I had prayed fervently that some wild beast might eat him, just as had befallen Silência. But now, before that sudden display of humility, I relented, overcome by remorse.

Father, please don't go on this hunt!

He looked at me over his shoulder with an astonishment that gradually turned into helpless sadness:

Why are you asking me this, Mariamar?

It's because I had a dream, Father. I dreamed of the sea.

Genito Mpepe was an expert in premonition. This ability to see ahead was what made him an excellent tracker. The future slipped through his dreams and the following day there was nothing that could take him by surprise. How was it that this time he was ignoring what to me was such an obvious omen?

You're only asking, Mariamar, because you're scared I'll kill your little huntsman. It's not me you want to protect.

Don't go, I beg you.

I have to go. I can't turn back. Those men have already paid me.

He turned around and walked away, dragging his feet as if reluctant. He paused to look at the trunk of the tamarind tree. It was I who broke the silence:

I was so sad when that tree died.

Then my father told me: When I got sick in my legs, it was my mother who cured me. It wasn't the mission, it wasn't Father Amoroso. My mother performed *takatuka* on me. She transferred my pain to that tree, which afterward couldn't stand the burden and withered away. That's what *takatuka* consists of: to switch someone's illness to something. That's what happened with me: Hanifa Assulua swapped my soul's injuries for the life of that tamarind. That's what my father told me as he said goodbye.

The Hunter's Diary

The Living Bone of a Dead Hyena

An army of sheep led by a lion is capable of defeating an army of lions led by a sheep.

— AFRICAN PROVERB

The administrator is impatient. "Operation Lion," as he now calls the hunt, is taking time to produce results. In the meantime, he has received an ultimatum from his superiors in the party. Outside investment in the region could be at risk if this area of tension is not resolved.

I even thought of drafting a report, saying everything was all right.

A false report?

It's what we subalterns do. We never say there's a problem. If we admit there's a problem, then that only brings more problems from our superiors. But Naftalinda read the report and threatened to expose its falseness publicly.

So that's why there's only one solution, my dear huntsman: Hurry up and kill these lions for me.

Not long after Florindo has left, there's a knock on the door from his well-endowed wife, Naftalinda. She asks whether the administrator has been here. Then she calls me over and whispers in my ear:

Florindo's in a hurry. He wants the matter brought to a conclusion. He's ordered arms to be distributed among the others. Be careful, my friend. There are people here who want to kill you.

That same afternoon, I set off alone. I make for the forests that line the road leading to Palma. I have a hunch that my walk may prove productive.

My hunch is proved right. After half an hour, the outline of a lioness emerges on the other side of a dried-up stream. The animal doesn't seem surprised, as if she were expecting this encounter. Without any warning, she lunges forward on the attack and in a split second covers the distance that separates us. More unexpected than the lioness's charge is my own shriek:

God help me!

That frenzied invocation is all I have left as the trigger awaits the pressure of my finger. What curse is it that weighs upon me as I commend my soul instead of firing a shot? Within me, my mother's prophecy and my father's inheritance vie with each other.

But lo and behold, suddenly the lioness stops her onward rush. Who knows, maybe she is surprised not to see me run away, terrified. She stops in front of me, her eyes fixed on mine. She is puzzled by me. I'm not what she expected. At that same moment, she ceases to be a lioness. When she withdraws, she has already left her existence. She is no longer even a living creature.

I arrive at our encampment in such a state of defeat and emptiness that I lie down on the veranda, prepared to sleep out in the open. I had the lioness in my sights and I failed like a novice, seized by fear. I don't deserve a roof over my head. Maybe the gods will find it easier to forgive me if I am modest and unprotected like this.

I'm not one of those people who seek help from the heavens when they are afflicted. As for praying, I only pray when I'm asleep. My dreams are my only prayers. I hope God doesn't take this badly. But it's just that all I have left is a tiny, temporary soul. Only at night does my spirit come alive, whispering softly so that no one may hear me. I ask for forgiveness for my descent into animality. But having a soul is a burden that I would only be able to bear when dead. That's why I loved so much, in so many deluded love affairs. That's why I hunt. To empty myself. To free myself from being a man.

The perfect opportunity, missed through my own fault, remains an obsession in my memory. The lioness continues before me, appraising my soul. There is a divine light in her eyes. I am beset by the strangest of thoughts: that somewhere, I have already contemplated those eyes that seem capable of hypnotizing a blind man.

A gentle weariness enfeebles my body; I'm assailed by the same anguish that causes moths to flutter helplessly around the oil lamp. I fall asleep. And I dream. I'm the opposite of the traditional hunter who, the night before, dreams of the animal he's going to kill. In my case, I dream of myself, gaining life only after having been killed by the creatures of the wild. These beasts are now my private monsters, my favorite works of creation. They will never cease to be mine, never stop moving through my dreams. Because I am, after all, their docile prisoner.

Kulumani's old church emerges in my dream. When I open its rust-hinged doors, I come face-to-face with a white priest. He is Portuguese, his face is familiar. It's hard to imagine his being a priest. His disheveled hair, his torn, dirty cassock, lend him the appearance of a beggar.

Come in, my son, he invites me. *My flock has been fervently awaiting you for so long. Archangel is your name and it was God who sent you.*

My eyes get used to the shadows: Those whom the priest calls his flock of believers are, in fact, lions and lionesses. These felines are sitting respectfully, listening with human devotion to the message that the priest is propagating from the pulpit. And together, priest and believers pray that I may be successful in my mission: that I may put an end to the brutalities of men who are pursuing innocent lions. The priest raises the chalice: *This is your blood*, he proclaims. Struggling to control themselves, the lions cover the church pews with their saliva. His arms outstretched, his voice battling in order not to be drowned by the roars of the wild animals, the missionary announces:

You haven't come to kill a lion. You've come to kill a person!

What a hell of a dream, I think as I awaken. I tell the writer about the ghosts that torment me at night. Gustavo smiles and remarks: *It's curious how we always dream of the same animals: lions, tigers, eagles, serpents. Deep down, we want to be those that can devour us.*

First thing in the morning, accompanied by the writer and by the tracker Mpepe, I set off for the arid wastelands that lie to the north of the village. The lions were prowling around there last night. I was confident that it would be easy to follow them: Over the wide area of sand, lions leave perfectly distinguishable tracks. This whole territory is called Kuva Vila. And it's true: In Shimakonde, the term means "empty." The place is deserted, godforsaken. It is said that not a drop of rain has ever fallen there, even in distraction.

We haven't been going for long before we catch sight of a solitary hyena in the distance. It walks along like a mirage against the indistinct background of the sand. The writer has difficulty in picking out the animal. Then, when he glimpses the prey, his face is lit with the incandescence of a moment, the flash of his senses. Afterward I explain to him: This is the real nature of my vice. It's not killing that fascinates me. It's this encounter with an elusive miracle, the fleeting and unrepeatable moment. All of a sudden I'm jolted by Genito Mpepe's explicit order:

Shoot, kill it!

Kill a hyena?

Can't you see? It's carrying something in its mouth; it looks like a piece of a leg.

I fear my fingers are going to disobey me yet again. But this time the rifle is true to its death-dealing nature. My shot is on target and the creature falls, its life erased. All this suddenly puzzles me. Why was I in control of my own fingers this time? The memory of my mother, soiled with my blood, as if she were giving birth to me a second time, surfaces once again. Once again, I hear her prophecy: It was not my fate to be a hunter. But then why should this premonition only manifest itself now?

Great shot, it was killed outright! the tracker rejoices.

But the truth is that for the first time, I fired without emotion, without soul: The shot tore through the silence without my being aware of having pulled the trigger.

When I bend over the prey, I see it has a bone in its mouth. It's not easy to free it from its powerful jaws. There's no doubt: It's a human femur. The creature has unearthed it, scratching around in these sinister sands.

Do you know what this means? Genito asks. *It means that the lions killed another person.*

When we arrive back in Kulumani, a crowd is gathering in front of the administration building. They've heard the shot and are awaiting some good news. But they are immediately disappointed when they identify what we're carrying in the back of the jeep.

This hyena belongs to someone, the blind man in the military tunic whispers in my ear.

There's immediate agreement: That animal wasn't reacting to its instinct. What it was doing was carrying out contract work. No one, much less an animal, goes snuffling around in the forbidden ground of Kuva Vila. It has been known since time immemorial that nothing was buried there except for the remains of old warriors. From the epic contests whose roll call grew longer over time: the wars against the *ngunis,* the German wars, the war against the Portuguese army, the civil war, and other domestic wars that never merited a name.

————

It's decided that the fateful bone should be taken to an old sorceress called Apia Nwapa. A bone doesn't appear out of nowhere. All the more serious when, as in this case, the bone really had appeared out of nowhere. I refuse to consult the spirits. I haven't got time for such distractions. But the writer insists that the visit is crucial and I mustn't try to sneak out of the need to accompany those participating in the ceremony. That way I would benefit from other blessings for the success of this mission.

I'm going to ask the river's permission

The sorceress pulls her hat down over her face and, at that moment, she turns into a shadow. Apia Nwapa is swollen with pride: Outsiders (including a representative of the administrator himself) are seated before her.

The woman leans heavily against the trunk of a baobab. Her feet stretched out in front of her, she settles herself as if this were her own private church. She looks lingeringly at the writer, at me, and at Maliqueto Próprio. Then she once again announces:

To give you authorization to hunt, I must first ask the river's permission.

The river? I ask testily.

The river has its rules. The great ngwena *lives in the Lideia. You, sir, know this crocodile only too well . . .*

I know it?

It's the same crocodile you, sir, killed a long time ago.

I can't avoid smiling. *Ngwena,* the crocodile? I already had a license to carry a gun—I was authorized to kill lions. Did I now have to await the decision of an imaginary crocodile? That's what I ask, half timidly, half incredulous. Apia's voice is contained, but she doesn't mince her words:

Imaginary? Do you doubt the crocodile? What sort of an African are you?

Let's leave my problems out of it. We came here for you to identify a bone found in a hyena's mouth.

The bone is laid at her feet. She doesn't move, but limits herself to contemplating the remains of the skeleton from a distance. She closes her eyes and inhales deeply as if she were assessing its smell.

This bone is still very much alive. The killing was done to order.

Bones are our only piece of eternity. The body goes, memories fade. The bones stay behind forever. These are Apia Nwapa's arguments: What we had in front of us wasn't just a femur. On the contrary, it was living proof of someone's existence.

Yes, but whose?

My mouth isn't suggesting anyone. You know whose it is.

Did we come here just to hear this? I ask defiantly.

Well, then, I'm going to suggest something, and you, sir, who are a hunter, are going to discover what lies behind my words. She pauses and, her eyes closed, adds: *A woman, lying on the ground, fell deeper than the dust. In the end, someone is going to get pregnant by a skeleton.*

Her message seems incomprehensible, but Maliqueto appears to understand its meaning perfectly clearly. Away from the witch's house, he calls us over to the edge of the road and explains:

That bone is Tandi's, the administrator's maid, the girl who was raped . . .

The cries in the village confirm the mourning: News of the latest victim of the killer lions has already spread. No one is surprised at it being Tandi. After she'd been raped, the girl had turned into a *vashilo*, one of those beings who sleepwalk through the night.

Exposed and alone like this, she surrendered to the voracious-
ness of the lions. Tandi had committed suicide.

When I turn in, the sobbing of the women can still be heard
in the streets. They weep for the person who has died. More
than her death, they sorrow over her brief, drab, meager life.
The witch's last words echo in my mind:

*Listen, hunter, it's not you who pull the trigger. The shot is fired by
another who, in that very instant, occupies your being.*

As far as I am concerned, that was the only time Apia Nwapa
told the truth.

The next morning, I visit Genito Mpepe. I clap my hands at the
entrance to the garden. It's his wife, Hanifa, who comes to the
door. The tracker, she tells me, has a hangover.

My husband is a kwambalwa, *she affirms. I could tell you he is
a drunkard. But what that man is can only be said in my language: a*
kwambalwa.

*All you can see, scattered around the garden over there, are flagons of
drink . . .*

*Don't be surprised, my good sir: I'm the one who prepares these flagons,
I'm the one who gives him his drink.*

For the women of Kulumani, a drunk is better than a husband. But in her case, the choice is between a serpent's spittle
and the devil's breath. In the end, Genito's violence when sober
is more painful than his cruelty when he's intoxicated.

Follow me, she says, leading me along pathways. *Come and see
how that man is still sleeping.*

Genito is curled up on a mat next to the well.

He's like an animal, Hanifa remarks. *Sometimes I pray to God that
he'll never wake up again,* she confesses.

I smile, embarrassed. I shake my head as if to relieve myself of the gravity of her declarations. But my hostess launches forth again, even more bitterly:

If he didn't wake up, I wouldn't have to kill him.

What's this, Hanifa?

That man gave me four daughters, but he's taken all of them away from me.

I was told the eldest was killed by lions.

It was Genito who killed her …

On that fateful morning, Silência was escaping from Kulumani, running away from Genito Mpepe's despotic regime.

Come and see her grave. It's right here, not far.

We cross some waste ground until we get to some nearby thickets. The grave is marked with a wooden cross and a large granite stone. Some wildflowers have been placed on this improvised gravestone. Some of them are still fresh.

Pretty flowers. Do you people bring them?

Us? You're the one who brings flowers.

Me?

Early each morning, you get down on your knees here and speak to the dead girl.

Hanifa leads me back to the house, while I am tormented by doubt: How was she able to invent a story about me bringing flowers for Silência? The woman's mad, I think.

In the yard, I hear someone cough behind a screen made of reeds. When I go to take a look, Hanifa pulls me by the arm and makes me sit down on the only chair.

It isn't anyone, only dogs. Those that haven't yet been eaten by the lions.

My hostess takes a pan of boiled sweet potato from the

kitchen and serves it on an earthenware plate. I'm not hungry, but I can't refuse. We share the food in silence.

I talk about killing Genito, but it's the whole of Kulumani that I'd like to get rid of.

Why are you so angry, Hanifa?

Here we are, the two of us, eating together. In Kulumani, that's forbidden. A man and a woman eating together? Only if the man is bewitched.

Who knows, maybe I am bewitched.

Suddenly I hear the noise of crockery falling from the thatch of a lean-to where it has been left to dry. And I see the shape of a woman rush by to hide behind the house.

Who is that?

It's no one.

But I saw her, I saw a woman hiding.

That's what I told you: Here, a woman is no one . . .

She gets up and without more ado leads me around to the front yard. It's a way of telling me that my visit is coming to an end. She wants to give me a few roots of manioc. I decline the gift gently. Before I leave, she takes my hands and asks:

You have such a deep sadness within you. What's the matter?

Nothing. Nothing's the matter. Why do you ask?

Why do you waste your time talking to a solitary old black woman like me?

Mariamar's Version

SIX

A River Without Sea

Wise is the firefly, for he uses the darkness to light up.
—A PROVERB FROM KULUMANI

On the night Archie arrived, I dreamed I was a hen languishing in Genito Mpepe's chicken coop. The other hens were my sisters. We lived a daily life shorn of history, like all those birds that are devoid of flight. In the meantime, we began to hear about chickens elsewhere who had turned into vultures. And we prayed that we would undergo the same metamorphosis. As vultures, we would ascend into the freedom of the skies and soar aloft in dizzying flight. But the miracle was long in coming.

One day, as he was feeding us corn, Grandfather Adjiru explained: It wasn't the mesh of the chicken coop that was separating us from freedom. The secret of our submission lay somewhere else, and dwelled deep within us: Every morning, Genito Mpepe would hypnotize us. A finger swaying like a pendulum in front of our beak was enough to plunge us into immobility, dead to the world. And when one of us seemed to awaken to life, our owner would place our head under our wing, and we would immediately sink back into our endless lethargy.

The dream recurred on the following nights. It was as if dreams were trying to warn me of something. That something, I now know, was fear. And everything has become clear: It wasn't on some whim that Archie abandoned me. His disappearance can be explained by fear. What he suffered from was the age-old terror that underneath the lake's surface lurked monsters. The suspicion that, concealed under my placid appearance, there dwelled a beast that would devour him. That was Archie's fear.

The truth is that Archie hadn't been made to share his existence. The greatness of a hunter lies in his solitude. His attacks of panic, his cowardice, bear no witnesses. Only his victim knows of his weaknesses. That's why the hunter is in a desperate hurry to be free of his prey.

Sixteen years ago, when Archie Bullseye watched me dancing at the village festival, he was already troubled by uncertainty. The hunter was afraid of what my body seemed to be saying, he was scared of whoever was speaking through my body while the drums beat. For him, ignorant of this language, it could only be dark forces. Demons speak like that, without words, saying everything through the body's carnality. This was his fear. But it wasn't demons who were making my body quiver. It was gods that speak and listen within us women. Archie's fear was the same as that of all men. That the time might return when we women were divinities. On getting entangled with me, with the gentleness of a light breeze, Archie wanted the protection and the blessing of these entities. But our gods are not the same. His slept inside books. Mine awoke with music. That's what the hunter didn't understand. I wasn't dancing. I was doing something else: I was freeing myself from time and responsibility, just as a snake sheds its old skin.

The Devil

What was happening to me now in this imposed confinement had already happened to me before. Sixteen years ago, when Archie Bullseye left the village, I lay on the veranda and watched the days go by. I was undergoing the same constriction that butterflies experience at a certain time. I was migrating into a chrysalis, wrapped in time and waiting for another creature to emerge from within me. Seeing me defeated and cowed, under the porch of our house, everyone assumed I'd returned to my paralysis of old. But my feeling of emptiness was only an appearance. For I knew that, though ephemeral, Archangel Bullseye's love had borne fruit. I waited until my belly had become rotund, and on the very day of my seventeenth birthday, I appeared before my mother with an air of triumphant defiance.

So you thought I wasn't a woman? Put your hand here, feel what I'm carrying inside me.

Her arm felt feeble in my hand and drooped even before touching my belly.

Have you heard a thunderclap and thought it's already raining, Mariamar? Well, there's still many a knot in the thread of time.

I don't understand, Mother.

I was lying. I knew what she was insinuating. The women of Kulumani, in each month of pregnancy, tie a knot in a piece of string that is passed from generation to generation.

We are women, she said. *We were made to overcome suffering.*

Not another word after that. Only an enigmatic smile that bordered on scorn. Without saying anything, my mother was scratching at an old wound: I was barren, my aridity had no cure.

Don't look at me like that, my daughter. You know very well whose fault it is.

There was no doubt: I was prevented from becoming a mother because of the beating I'd had from my father. Even the nurse had confirmed the grave consequences of all those kicks.

There are children who are born and die within us, Hanifa affirmed, putting an end to the conversation.

These were words written by the hand of fate. For on that very night, I was woken from sleep by a nightmare: Deep inside me, a carnivorous beast was devouring my baby. My mulatto baby, my impure child, conceived on the road, was vanishing like a dream in the darkness. I awoke with a start, my sheet was wet: Blood was visiting me, turning my thighs red. I screamed, insulting my mother, shouting that I was giving birth. That blood on the bed was a creature, a living clot of plasma, a blood-person.

This is my son, this is your grandson, I shouted, my open hands dripping, red and viscous, as Hanifa Assulua entered my room.

Today, I know: The story of my childhood is no more than a half-truth. In order to deny a half-truth one needs far more than the whole truth. That huge truth, so vast that I couldn't capture it, was only one truth: It wasn't the physical punishments that made me sterile. That was the more palatable version invented by my mother. The crime was another one: For years, my father, Genito Mpepe, abused his daughters. First, it happened with Silência. My sister put up with it quietly, without sharing this terrible secret. The moment my breasts began to show, I was the victim. At the end of the day, Genito would migrate away from himself by means of *lipa*, the palm liquor. After he'd drunk his fill, he would come into our room and the nightmare would begin. The incredible thing was that, at the moment of rape, I exiled myself, incapable of being the person lying there under my father's sweating body. Through some strange process, I managed to forget straight afterward what I had been through. This sudden amnesia had one purpose to it: to avoid my becoming an orphan. In the end, everything that occurred never got as far as actually happening: Genito Mpepe escaped to another existence and I turned into another creature who was inaccessible and nonexistent.

My mother, Hanifa Assulua, always pretended she didn't know anything. It was the neighbors' invention, the frenzy of those wishing to hide their own ills. When the evidence overwhelmed her, she summoned me and asked, her voice trembling:

Is it true?

I didn't answer, my gaze fixed on the ground. My silence, as far as she was concerned, was confirmation:

A curse on you, you hussy!

Without reacting at all, I saw her jump on me, attacking me with her fists and feet, insulting me in her mother tongue. What she said, amid all her spitting and foaming, was that it was my fault. It was all my fault. Even though Silência had warned her: It was I who provoked her man. She didn't refer to Genito as my father. He was now "her man."

Get out of this house. I never want to see you here again.

I never got as far as leaving. On the contrary, I shut myself away between the walls, so much so that no one had ever become so cloistered inside a house. Hanifa Assulua summoned a witch doctor and this *uwavi* made me drink a bitter potion. For a whole day I took it from a little clay pot. The following day, the poison had worked. I had turned into a body without a soul. Instead of blood, I had a venomous sap: That's what remained in my veins.

My mother was getting her revenge: Before, she had transferred my illness to the tree in our yard. Now she was carrying out *takatuka* in reverse: She was displacing my life to the dead tree. And in an instant it was reborn, proud and verdant. I, on the other hand, turned into an inanimate creature. I only had one faculty left: I had the power of hearing. For the rest, I was surrounded by some ancient, congenital darkness.

What Hanifa Assulua intended was more than my physical elimination. Dying was the least of it. My very birth had to be erased. The dead aren't absent: They remain alive, they speak to us in our dreams, they weigh upon our conscience. The punishment reserved for me was complete and utter exile. Not from Kulumani, but exile from my reason and from language. I was declared mad. Madness is the only perfect absence. In my insanity I was visible, but shut away; sick but without any wound; hurt but without any pain.

My grandfather Adjiru attempted to save me, and tried out his own *mintela*. But it was in vain. Father Amoroso was called. But this time the Portuguese priest was unable to bring about a miracle. *Take her to the hospital straightaway* was all he had to say. They took me to Palma and the nurse produced a diagnosis without even batting an eyelid: These things have no cause.

With some luck, she'll walk again.

I stayed in the infirmary for some time without showing any sign of improvement. Medicine gave up on me, but that wasn't why they left me there. I remained in the hospital at Palma, lifeless, and with even less company. It was only later that I understood why my return to Kulumani had been delayed. My grandfather Adjiru died during that time. They didn't want me to be present. Not to save me from having to say farewell. But in order that my farewell should last a lifetime.

On the first anniversary of my grandfather's death, they took me to visit his grave. The deceased had left an express wish that he wanted me to be present at the ceremony. I had already returned home, but my condition hadn't altered. No one wanted to carry me along the road in such a state. I might contaminate the vehicles. They chose to take me down the river in a boat, as far as the sacred wood that was the resting place of Adjiru and my great-grandfather Muarimi.

With the strength of their arms they deposited me in the craft. At that moment, my body rolled over and I fell, helpless, into the waters of the River Lideia. They say I disappeared down to the deep riverbed and remained immersed for a long time. When they eventually pulled me out, I wore the mesmerized expression of the newly born. Gradually I appeared before the eyes of the world. I took a few staggered steps around me, shook my shoulders as if freeing myself from an invisible burden. There was no doubt, according to the family's chorused testimony:

Mariamar has returned! Mariamar has returned!

I was the focus of their astonished looks. I was the center of the universe. Silence fell, my family waiting for what would come next.

Where are my sisters? These were my first words.

They brought forward Silência, my eldest sister, and the little twins, Uminha and Igualita. In silence, I kissed Silência and knelt down to look at my youngest sisters. In my own mind, only a few months had passed. But the girls were sadly old. I always wondered whether there were ever any children in Kulumani. Can one call a child a creature who cultivates the soil, chops firewood, carries water, and at the end of the day doesn't have anyone to play with?

Suddenly my father broke the silence, put an end to our hugs, and declared:

We're going to see the ocean.

The ocean? my mother answered, astonished.

The whole family's going, Genito Mpepe exclaimed peremptorily. *That's what I promised your grandfather.*

It wasn't to the ocean that I wanted them to take me. All I wanted was to return to my mother's arms, for her to lull me, and for me to be a little girl again. That was the only ocean I wanted. That's when I understood why Father Amoroso spoke so often of the final deluge. That's what I yearned for: a flood that might wipe away this world. This world that forced a woman like Hanifa to have children, but that didn't allow her to be a mother; that forced her to have a husband, but didn't allow her to know love.

The whole family was enraptured by the sight of the ocean in all its vastness, its living infinity, its unlimited horizon that seemed to originate in our very selves. My sisters, benumbed with astonishment, were lost for words, infatuated by such immensity. I was the only one to walk down to the shoreline. What fascinated me wasn't this absence of limits. I was enchanted by the foam, the shreds of spume that were released from the crest of the waves. Like white birds, without weight or wings, these scraps would launch into fanciful flight only to dissolve in the air. I rolled the word "spume" on my lips and uttered it a thousand times. If one day I were to have a daughter, I would call her Spume.

The name I chose for this unimaginable child is, after all, the right one. For my descendants will be forged out of the same matter that is released from the waves and flutters away until it is no more than a void. I shall never have children, I shall never have anyone to give a name to.

And yet, every new moon I suffer spasms, and in the solitude of my bed, I give birth. Dozens of children, I've had dozens of children, no other woman has given birth so many times. Babies without number have been born and every one of them has become extinguished a moment later like a shooting star crossing the skies. My hopeless children have vanished away, but the true pains of those hopeless births will haunt me for the rest of my life.

My mother, Hanifa Assulua, who knows about suffering, gave me sound advice: Pains pass, but they don't disappear. They migrate into us, come to rest somewhere in our being, submerged in the depths of a lake.

The Hunter's Diary

SIX

The Reencounter

I'm only happy before I live. I only recall within my dreams. That is why I write.

—EXTRACT PILFERED FROM THE WRITER'S NOTEBOOKS

Tandi is buried early in the morning. There aren't many people at her funeral. Most of them are women. The administrator puts in an appearance, accompanied by his wife. The deceased was, after all, their maid. The absence of her boss would provoke suspicion in the village. In contrast to her husband, Naftalinda looks shattered. At one point she tries to make a speech. But her sobs prevent her from speaking. She composes herself, wipes away her tears, and gradually assumes a pose of majestic grandeur:

The lions are besieging the village and the men continue to send the women out to look after the allotments, continue to send their daughters and wives to collect firewood and water in the early morning. When are we going to say no? When there are none of us left?

She hoped the other women would respond to her invitation to rebel. But they shrug their shoulders and walk off, one by one. The First Lady is the last woman to abandon the ceremony. Deep inside her, she feels like the very last woman. Just as I feel like the last hunter.

When the service is over, Florindo comes up to me to announce that rifles will arrive the following day.

You're going to have reinforcements.

I don't need any. All I need is me. Keep the weapons for something else. To combat poachers, for example.

Maliqueto and Genito are going to get weapons and will be under your command.

I'm not going to command anyone. If you want to form another team, that's fine. But what I've got to do, I shall do by myself.

The discussion gets more heated. Those present move away as a sign of disapproval. This is not the appropriate time or place. But the administrator is too excited:

Do you realize the political risk I'm taking? That I staked everything on this hunting expedition for my promotion? What is it you want me to do, to get involved in other procedures?

The writer draws us away, far from the church. It's he who resumes the conversation:

I don't understand, my dear Makwala. What do you mean by "other procedures"?

To tell you the truth, the administrator replies, *I'm beginning to have my doubts about these lions. Because they come into the village, even during the day, and their intentions are almost human...*

The writer laughs, but Florindo doesn't give up: These animals are looking for someone, sniffing around doors, they are killing to order. They can only be fabricated lions: Why else would they not eat the poisoned meat left out for them before as bait? And why did they tear up clothes left out on the clotheslines?

You can be sure of this: No true lion would behave like this, the administrator concludes emphatically.

When we get back to our quarters, I prepare lunch. The writer is in the living room, working. I notice he keeps peering at my chaotic papers. I don't care anymore. I also read his notebooks and even steal the odd sentence of his. On the other hand, I'm beginning to get a somewhat tardy taste for writing. Something about the act of writing suggests the pleasure of hunting to me: In the emptiness of the page, there are infinite shocks and surprises concealed.

I serve Gustavo his lunch and fill his glass. The writer begins to feel uncomfortable with such ceremony. During our meal, neither of us exchanges a word. Afterward, I go to my room and return with a rifle that I throw abruptly into his arms.

What's this, Archie?

It's yours. The rifle is all yours.

Please, Archie, what the hell do I want with this filthy weapon?

I raise the palm of my hand as a sign for him to listen, without any interruptions.

Do you remember what happened that night when Hanifa called us? Do you remember how I hesitated to pull the trigger?

The writer places the weapon on the floor with the utmost care, as if he were handling an explosive device. I wait for him to finish this delicate operation before going on:

Some days ago, Gustavo, you wanted to know which hand I used to shoot. Well, I use neither the right nor the left hand. I no longer shoot.

I don't understand.

My fingers don't obey me anymore—my fingers have died. The truth is this: I can no longer hunt.

I hold my arms up high, displaying my fingers, which are crooked like old hooks. The writer is lost for words. I have come across as being so sincere, so vanquished, that he can't come to terms with seeing his image of me crumble before his eyes.

I've lost my hands, I conclude, defeated.

I observe my hands as if I'd never seen them before, as if they were completely strange. In exactly the same way as my brother Roland had contemplated his useless body in the hospital.

Don't tell anyone, I beg in a whisper.

No one will know, Gustavo assures me. Then he asks: *Forgive me, but wouldn't it be better to accept the administrator's offer and hunt with the help of Genito and Maliqueto?*

Never.

I don't understand. So who is going to kill the lions?

You.

How?

You're the one who's going to kill them.

You're crazy!

I'll lead you, don't worry. At the precise moment, all you have to do is pull the trigger.

I expected the man to be more obdurate and refuse flat-out. But Gustavo Regalo seems to be pondering. Maybe the writer is beginning to yield to a surreptitious desire. He picks up the gun, weighs it in his hands, and aims at an imaginary target.

Do you think I could hit the creature? he asks.

There's a glimmer of a new emotion in the writer's soul. There's the beginning of an almost infantile enthusiasm. And I think: Everything that we have carefully built over centuries in order to remove ourselves from our animal nature, everything that language has covered over with metaphors and euphemisms (our arms, our faces, our waists), in one instant can be converted back to its naked, brutish substance: flesh, blood, bone. The lion doesn't just devour people. It devours our very humanity.

And if I miss? Gustavo wants to know.

Don't worry, my dear writer. I'm not giving you the gun to kill the lion. It's more for you to defend me.

I hope the writer will defend me. It looks as if he's already started defending someone: He has sent a report to the central government criticizing Florindo's inertia with regard to the rape of Tandi.

Have you spoken to Naftalinda? I ask.

It was she in fact who asked me to denounce this crime. And Hanifa, the maid, also came to me: She maintained that it was her husband, Genito Mpepe, who was in charge of the gang of rapists.

Do you trust what Hanifa says after that episode the other night?

Genito Mpepe himself confessed he was in the mvera *leading those fiends.*

My dream about the lions in the church springs to my mind. And I remember Father Amoroso's strange prophecy: *You haven't come to hunt lions. You've come to kill a person!*

Tandi's funeral, so simple and poorly attended, worried me more than I could have imagined. I wasn't allowed to attend the funerals of my mother and father. I wasn't the right age. I don't know whether there's a right age to contemplate death. Tandi's disappearance affected me as if some part of me had been torn away. I had held one of that woman's bones in my hand. How can I sleep without being visited by ghosts?

The ceiling slowly gains density and I slip into a rare and mellow state of sleepiness. On that border between wakefulness and slumber, that's when I see my sister-in-law enter my room, with the wariness of a shadow. I'm dreaming, and I don't want to leave my dream. Luzilia emerges from the mist, Luzilia creeps through the house, Luzilia slips into my sleeping quarters. Beautiful, sweet-smelling, suggestive. She seizes the rifle and begins to dance with it. She caresses the weapon as if acquiring life from it. I sit there motionless, and follow her sinuous insinuations. The woman brushes the barrel of the rifle across her face as she stares at me, weighing me up with her eyes.

Be careful, it's loaded! I warn her.

I know, that's why I'm dancing with it.

All dances are like this one, dangerous, almost fatal, the nurse adds. *We start off in the arms of life, and end up dancing with death.*

Her lips kiss the trigger and then she sucks the barrel lasciviously. Her eyes remain fixed on mine. But I sit there, cold and distant. It's well known: There's a time to love and there's a time to hunt. The two never mix. If I were to give in, I would be betraying an age-old tradition: When one is hunting, one cannot have sex.

Don't you see, Archie? I'm the lame serpent . . .

Then I understand: The woman wanted to take possession of

my soul. To my astonishment, Luzilia begins to take off her clothes, her body emerging leisurely and voluptuous. The light that bathes her gives her a moonlit air of unreality. She approaches, turns her back, and leans against me, impressing upon me her bodily curves. The ice turns to boiling water in my heart: I unravel, excited to the marrow, unable to speak, my fire quickened.

Have you nothing to say, my little Archangel? she asks.

What she asks is too hard a task. I am the hostage of temptation: When I try to speak, I lose my throat; when I try to touch her, my fingers fail me. Exactly as happened while hunting, in love too I am no longer in control of my body. All that I can utter is an inarticulate puff:

Say, me?

All at once she faces me. Her mouth, her teeth, her tongue, everything in her joins forces to extract my soul. And I almost die at long last, plunging into the abyss of sleep.

I awaken with a jolt and walk along the hall when the first shreds of light herald the new morning. I pass the writer, who announces point-blank:

A woman has just left here.

A woman? What woman?

I don't know, I've never met her before. She arrived from Maputo, she's come looking for you. She says her name is Luzilia.

Luzilia?

Impassive on the surface, a volcano within me: Here I am, caught by surprise like an ambushed animal. In my outward air I am serene, but within me I am running impetuously, an adolescent succumbing to temptation. And I can already feel Luzilia's body next to mine, already am absorbed in her groans and her sighs. It isn't just the fulfillment of a dream I am seeking, but the healing of a wound caused by rejection.

An hour later, Luzilia returns. She greets me with a kiss on the cheek that almost brushes my lips. She pats her face, scratched by the rough brush of my unshaven chin. I feel her breasts touching my chest, and we remain like that for a moment or two.

I knew you'd come.

Liar. I didn't even know myself.

So how's my brother?

It's because of him that I'm here. Your brother . . . I don't know how to tell you . . .

Has he died?

No, not yet.

Not yet?

Roland wants you to return to Maputo as quickly as you can. There are things he wants to tell you before he dies.

I need one more day. Then we can go back together.

Well, then, I'll go back to Palma, as I'm in a guesthouse there. Meet me there tomorrow.

Don't go just yet, Luzilia. I want to show you the river. Afterward, I'll drive you back to Palma.

From the most prominent bank of the Lideia we contemplate the valley in absolute silence. Only after we have sat down on the granite rocks does the nurse get ready to talk:

There are things I have to tell you. First, about your mother, about her death.

I know what happened. She was ill.

Your mother died of kusungabanga.

Is that the name of an illness?

You could say that. An illness that kills all the others, those who aren't ill.

At first I didn't understand. But then Luzilia explained: In the language of Manica, the term *kusungabanga* means to close with a knife. Before migrating for work, there are men who sew up their wife's vagina with needle and thread. Many women get infected. In the case of Martina Bullseye, her infection proved fatal.

Roland knew about it. That's why he killed his father. It wasn't an accident. He avenged his mother's death.

My heart is flooded with anger: My brother had killed my father! And I repeat "my father" to myself as if he were more mine than Roland's. My accusation gradually gives way to another feeling akin to envy.

Tell me, Luzilia: Can my brother sleep?

Roland sleeps, his wife confirms. How could I remain indifferent? My brother had managed the total exile that I had always coveted. I envied Roland for his madness and his slumber. I envied him for his wife, and the love given him that I never had.

I walk away from Luzilia, over to the cliff to get a better view of the valley. Ever since I arrived in Kulumani, the waters of the river have swollen. In the distant mountains where it rises, it must have begun to rain. The river never sleeps. In this, it's like me...

Here by the river, I courted a girl...

I use the vague memory like a rapier, moved by the absurd wish to hurt Luzilia. And I continue:

There were two sisters, that's right, but I can't remember their names or their faces. I got as far as kissing one of them. But I don't remember either of them. Maybe if I saw them again...

Men, men! A woman would never forget like that. I bet they remember you.

I admit that at the time I was drinking heavily and even resorted to the liquors they make around here.

So what had you come to do here, in the back of beyond?

I'd come to kill a dangerous crocodile.

And did you succeed?

Do you doubt my skill as a hunter?

You didn't always catch what you wanted.

I pretend not to hear. I follow the example of feline creatures, who feign distraction before hurling themselves at their prey. I no longer know how to deal with Luzilia except as a hunter.

There's one thing I don't understand. Is it true that you understand what Roland is saying in that strange way of talking he has?

Suddenly I realize how close I am to my father's suspicions when confronting the fidelity of my mother's letters. My God, how like Henry Bullseye I am! Luzilia is far from my thoughts when she replies:

Don't forget I'm a nurse. And then I've been looking after him for so long! I listen to your brother like someone reading another person's palm.

Nor should I forget that Roland could make use of the written word. It had always been his weapon, his refuge. From her trousers pocket, Luzilia draws two sheets of paper. She chooses the most crumpled one and gives it to me. It's a letter from Roland, I recognize the handwriting of the well-behaved, eternal child. I don't like reading out loud. I feel weak, ridiculous, denuded. For that reason, I read it in an undertone.

My dear brother: I imagine my condition must pain you. I want to tell you that I don't suffer. On the contrary, I'm happy because I can never again be a Bullseye. I have shed my inherited name with the same pleasure that some widows burn the clothes of their tyrant husband. After that shot, I no longer feared what I had been. No further crime awaits me. I am empty, like only a saint can be. Do you remember what our mother would call us? My angels, that's what she would say. Here in this asylum, there's no need for demons or angels. All we have is ourselves, and that's enough. Yes, I killed our father. I killed him and will kill him again every time he's reborn. I obey orders. Those orders were given me without the need for any words. It was enough to see my mother's sad look. Don't pity me, dear brother. At first, my alibi was madness. Then, it became my absolution. Our mother always warned me: A bullet kills in both directions. When I killed old Bullseye, I committed suicide. Once, after our mother's death, you said: If only I could die. Well, now I'm telling you. It's not death that confers absence upon us. The only way to cease existing is to go mad. Only a madman gains vacuity.

Those lines confirmed my age-old suspicion: My brother pretended he was mad. The only truly sick creature was me, with my tormented nights, and my cruel memories of a half-lived past.

Can I ask another question? Did you and my brother ever make love?

Luzilia doesn't answer. She merely smiles sadly. She unfolds the second sheet and waves it in front of me.

Do you recognize this?

It's my old letter, that unlucky missive in which, many years ago, I declared my love. Without saying any more, Luzilia walks toward me, her sad smile now taking on an enigmatic air. She kisses me.

Let's go to Kulumani, let's go to your room.

We can't. The writer shares the space with me.

Let's go to Palma, we'll be more relaxed there.

We get into the car. Her hand stops me from turning the ignition. And she whispers in my ear:

You were right, this is your last hunt. I'm coming to get you . . .

We set off in silence, Luzilia's hand still perched on my arm.

Tonight . . . And she pauses, seeking the right word.

Yes?

Tonight, make me scared of myself.

I look at the sandy road that unfolds in front of us, with more bends in it than distance, and I think: To live is to wait in hope of what may be lived.

Mariamar's Version

The Ambush

Be careful of lions. But be more careful of the goat that lives in the lion's den.

—AFRICAN PROVERB

Ever since the hunter arrived, the days have gone by, dense but empty like the clouds in winter. During this whole time, I have remained shut away, a prisoner in my own home, peeping out at the failed preparations for the hunting expeditions. I heard my father's footsteps echoing through the early hours of the morning and the noise of the jeep would have me throwing myself at the window to get a glimpse of Archie Bullseye.

Little by little, though, my interest in my beloved began to fade. Why didn't he send me some sign that he might be interested in seeing me again? There was only one true answer: I had died as far as he was concerned. There was no point in prolonging the illusion. It was this profound deception that made me give up. I no longer wanted to escape from the house; I could forgo a meeting with the hunter. I could do without the river, travel, dreams.

I wasn't the only one disappointed in Archie Bullseye. The village elders were impatient, and began to hold meetings in the *shitala*, while an atmosphere of conspiracy began to take a grip on Kulumani. Florindo Makwala, the administrator, began to be seen at these meetings of the elders. His presence there was something unheard-of in the village. Makwala had always drawn a line between himself and the world that he called "traditional," had always distanced himself from engaging with invisible matters. That was why people were puzzled by his sudden interest.

This afternoon, something unexpected happens. The administrator, Florindo Makwala, comes to our house. It's not the custom for chiefs to leave their residence in order to discuss matters of governance. But this time Makwala has come to ask for favors. Shut away in the living room, he and my father confer for some time. I begin to fear that I may be the subject of negotiation. This fear is confirmed when I am later summoned to receive a disturbing command:

Tonight, you're to go with the administrator! Genito Mpepe declares.

But aren't I in prison? I ask.

You're going to sleep over there, in his house, my father affirms, embarrassed.

In the visitor's presence I manage to contain myself, though deep down I feel annihilated. The moment Florindo leaves, however, my entreaty gushes out:

Father, don't do this to me. For the love of God, I don't want to—

What you want has nothing to do with it.

But, ntwangu, *please, think carefully,* my mother declares, unexpectedly taking up my defense. *That Florindo, that miserable worm . . .*

Mpepe won't brook any dissent. We should keep quiet. Did we know that, at the dead of night, there were conspiracies against his person? Did we realize how weak and isolated he was? Doing the administrator favors was his golden opportunity to regain his protection and respect.

In silence, my mother prepares my bath, dresses me, and combs my hair. The sun is starting to go down when she escorts me to Florindo Makwala's residence. She stands in the road without moving as she watches me enter the garden, and even calls me:

Your scarf, girl . . .

And she passes her hand over my face, pretending to tidy my hair. She lingers, gripped by her very gesture. She takes her time looking at me before saying:

Don't worry, my girl, you're very pretty.

And she sets off home. I stand there alone, undecided, at the entrance of what the administrator always insisted was not a "house" but a "residence." My hesitation is brief: The administrator comes to greet me at the door and invites me into his office. There's a large sofa that he promptly occupies while I look around at the walls, where there's a huge calendar with a Chinese woman lying lecherously across the hood of a car.

The photo of His Excellency is missing because your mother, Hanifa, was cleaning it and ended up breaking the glass. I'm awaiting funds to order a new frame . . .

I stand there waiting while he withdraws into himself, his head bowed over his knees.

I'm so desperate, Mariamar!

Soon, I think, he'll burst into tears. On a sudden maternal impulse, I sit down next to him, but then I remain motionless, as befits someone of my status.

Give me your hand, Florindo says.

Clumsy and confused, I stretch out my arm and half open my fingers. I stay like that for a while without him reacting to my gesture.

Do you know why you're here?

I lie, shaking my head timidly. A sour smell pervades the air around me. Florindo Makwala takes my hand and leads me across the room just as a married couple of many years' standing might do as they retire to their sleeping quarters. He leads me down a long dark corridor and, near the door at the end, places his head next to mine. I avoid him abruptly, but he persists and then whispers in my ear:

There's a problem with my wife, Naftalinda.

At last, he explains himself. The reason for my presence there is, after all, far removed from what I had suspected. In fact, the root of Florindo's despair lies elsewhere. His wife had offered herself as bait for the lions. Her husband had tried to dissuade her. In vain. The First Lady insisted that she would go and sleep naked, in the open air, night after night, until the lions were attracted and came and devoured her. This was her stated intention. Unless he, Florindo, behaved like a real man and assumed a firm position over the Tandi affair and so many other issues.

My wife, my one and only wife...

Naftalinda would neither look nor listen. The administrator was in a panic. It was crucial that Naftalinda should be distracted from her suicidal intention. The First Lady would only listen to someone like me, someone who lived in the same type of solitude, who spoke the same type of language.

Are you sure I'm the right person, sir? At home everyone says I'm not even a person...

The administrator is more than convinced. Naftalinda and I had much in common: We'd been born in the same year, we'd both studied at the mission, we were both condemned not to have children, destined never to be women.

Go into that room and speak to her. But there's one thing: Never address her by her old name. She doesn't like it now...

In Kulumani, we gain names depending on the time and how old we are. Oceanita was Naftalinda's first name, when she was just an infant, because of the volume of her tears. When she cried it was like the tide coming in. Each tear was a watery egg that fell on the ground with a loud splash.

The girl became a teenager and her body expanded in volume. Concerned, the family delivered her into the care of Father Amoroso: For so big a body, she would need many souls. We both met at the mission. My reason for being there was to cure my paralysis. Hers was to get lighter. I walked again. But she never shed any weight. In spite of a change in name, the girl remained fat. When we said goodbye to each other at the entrance to the mission, I noticed for the first time a bitterness in her look and a harshness in her voice:

Never call me Oceanita again. I'm Naftalinda now.

She was sent to the city and I heard no more about her until a few days ago, when she returned to Kulumani accompanying her husband and my hunter of lions. Ever since then, I hadn't seen her again unless it was from afar, when she made her triumphal incursion into the menfolk's *shitala*. As far as I was concerned, she was still Oceanita. But for all the others, she didn't need a name at all. She was merely a wife, a very special wife. She was the First Lady in a village without any ladies.

Now all the chief's voluminous spouse wants to do is die. It strikes me that her desire for suicide actually stems from a purely generous sentiment. She is so fleshy that the animals would feel sated and leave the village in peace for many a moon. Or who knows, maybe the hunters would take advantage of the moment to mount an ambush against the execrable beasts...?

The administrator opens the door with painstaking care and signals me to go in alone. I advance through the half-light, guided by the noise of heavy breathing. It's as if her exhaled breaths collapse, exhausted, from her ample chest, like injured birds plummeting from high cliffs.

Step by step, I identify shadows until at last I detect the First Lady's presence. She's seated like Buddha, in a big old chair, her fingers submerged in two glasses of vinegar.

It's to soften my nails, she announces, without greeting me.

Her screeching voice is like a nail scraping glass. She doesn't notice me quiver. Her gaze is concentrated on her own hands.

I adore my nails, she states, blowing on her fingers. And she adds: *They're the only thin part of my body.*

The whiff of vinegar adds flavor to an irrational fear that has assailed me ever since I entered the house. It's a trap, I think with a shudder. It's not the lion she wants to capture, but me. The inquisitorial gaze of my hostess comes to rest on me at last.

I've already forgiven you, my friend.

She is now confessing, so many years later: She'd always been envious of me, of my slim figure, my almond eyes. Her envy tormented her all the more every time I climbed up on the boys' backs and they ran off with me, falling to the ground with me as if we were one body, and laughing with me in one single whoop.

How I hated you, Mariamar! I prayed so often to God that he might take you away.

I was now more used to the light, and I contemplated her as thoroughly as a dockworker might inspect a cargo on the quay. My gaze probes her like a blind man. I stare at Oceanita without ever actually seeing her. Her invisible elbows, her moon-shaped dimples, her folds and tucks: The girl is a whole plantation of flesh. Then I realize: She finds my scrutiny irritating. When she tries to get up, she's like a star uncoupling from the universe.

I'll help you, I am quick to offer.

There's no need. She brushes me away energetically.

But then she falls back, as if her legs were failing her. And she uses me to support herself, like a ship nudging against the quay. She seems to get pleasure from this lingering touch. I maneuver her away with great care, and take a couple of steps back to contemplate her again. When some days before I glimpsed her from afar, I wasn't aware of her size. Now I realize: Naftalinda is so fat that even when she's standing, she's still lying down.

All of a sudden the woman lifts up her skirt, exhibiting her forbidden parts, and I quickly look away. But the First Lady stands there without moving, like a statue, exposing herself without any shame.

Take a good look at me! Don't be afraid to look, we're both women. How can a man desire me? How can I seduce Florindo, tell me?

Don't do this to me, I beg her.

What did Florindo tell you? Did he tell you I'd offered myself to be fed to the lions? Well, he didn't understand. I want to be devoured, but I want to be devoured in the sexual sense. I want a lion to make me pregnant.

A lion would burrow like a miner until it reached her core. That was her secret plan. I look at her. She has a pretty face; her eyes are deep-set, dream-laden.

Do you know something, Mariamar? I miss our time at the mission. The mission wasn't just a religious house: It was a country. Do you understand? We two lived in a foreign country. We're whiter than that Archangel fellow.

I help her back into the chair, and tell her I shall be spending the night with her, sharing her room just as we used to do at the mission.

Naftalinda?

Call me Oceanita...

Can I sleep in this corner?

Wherever you like, but first of all help me to go out, I want to fulfill my dream.

I can't. I promised I wouldn't let you go out.

I just want to go out and come back in again.

Let's go, then, but only for a bit. And only here, next to the house.

She takes me by the hand and leads me to the open ground in front of the administration building. Everyone in the village is asleep, and from the bushes all we can hear is the sad hoot of the nightjars. Naftalinda contemplates the darkened houses and laments:

I feel sorry for Florindo. He's a clown. He thinks that people venerate him. No one respects him, no one loves him.

She takes a few steps toward the bushes that surround the garden, chooses an old tree trunk, sits down on it, and remains in that position as if she were in prayer. Naftalinda falls asleep while I keep watch on her from a distance. Gradually I surrender to sleep until, in a split second, there is chaos and confusion: A rustling in the long grass, a low growl, and a shadow hurtles toward Naftalinda like a fireball. In a flash I see a lioness clutching her vast body and both of them, almost indistinct from one another, embracing in a deadly dance.

Help, a lioness! Help!

Yelling aloud, I rush forward to help the girl. The lioness is startled by my attack. With an impetus that I never guessed I was capable of, I grow in strength and size and force the lioness to back off. Here is an opportunity for Naftalinda to get away. But she rejects my help and runs to embrace her aggressor once again. In an instant, the three of us are rolling around together, there is a confusion of nails and claws, slobbering and panting, roars and screams. My frenzy causes my body to double in strength: I bite, scratch, kick. Surprised, the lioness eventually gives up. Defeated, she retreats with all the dignity of a queen dethroned. And she disappears into the darkness on the other side of the road.

For a few seconds, I remain on top of Naftalinda, but then suddenly the sky itself collapses on top of me. The pain is huge, I scream in despair, I turn on myself and catch a glimpse of Florindo with a stick raised above his head, ready to deliver the final blow.

It's me! It's me, Mariamar!

A chorus of voices breaks out: *Kill her, Florindo! That woman is the lioness herself!* The whole village throngs together around us, demanding justice. Next to me, Naftalinda is covered in blood. She gets up on her knees, opens her arms to protect my body, and proclaims in a kind of screech:

No one touch this woman. No one!

Still clutching the stick, Florindo Makwala, confused, orders the crowd back. He kneels down next to me to ask how I am. His voice is also on its knees as he murmurs:

I'm sorry, Mariamar, but in the darkness I didn't see it was you.

At first the people retreat. But then, of one voice, they begin to yell once more, demanding my immediate execution. And once again they advance in a frenzy. I'm assailed by the old dream, that I'm going to die as I always dreamed I would, flat-out on a stretch of beach, shapes hovering above me like vultures, ready to devour my soul. And the kicking and punching no longer hurt me, I don't hear the insults anymore, and I'm not even aware that the crowd is dispersing like an ocean wave. The person responsible for causing the crazed horde to melt away is Florindo Makwala, who has grown in both body and voice. Seen from down on the ground, he is like a mountain and his command is that of an irate demigod:

Back! Get back or I'll kill you with my own hands.

Astounded, Naftalinda looks at her husband as if she doesn't recognize him. Then she sighs:

My man, my man's come back!

The administrator stands there, statuesque and threatening, until suddenly we hear shots. At first far away. For a long moment the people are paralyzed between expectation and fear. Then there are more shots, this time nearer. The onlookers dash off in the direction of the road. It's not long before the sound of voices reaches us, excited but indistinguishable. It's Archie who's coming, I think. The hunter has come to rescue me—he's finally appeared before my weary heart. The cries are now clear:

They've killed the lions! They've killed the lions!

I get to my feet with difficulty and stagger toward the road. And there he is, my savior! His weapon over his shoulder, he stands out in the darkness and is walking toward me. But gradually the figure becomes clearer and I realize it's not Archie Bullseye. It's Maniqueto, the policeman. Surrounded by the crowd that welcomes him in all his glory, he brandishes the bloodied ear of the slaughtered lion in his right hand.

I killed this lion out there in the bush.

But we heard shots nearby . . .

The other one, the lioness, was killed right here, on the road.

He is greeted with euphoric applause. No one notices Florindo helping his injured wife back home. Only I haven't a home to go back to. Only I weep on the dark ground of Kulumani.

lioness was not killed ⟶

it was mortimer

rebellious spirit being killed.

The Hunter's Diary

The Demon Saint

Of bones and Sun, not of Life, is Time made. For Life is
made against Time. Without measurement, woven from
infirm infinities.

—EXTRACT PILFERED FROM THE WRITER'S NOTEBOOKS

I hear gunfire in the middle of the night. I feel like leaving
Palma, setting off down the road and discovering the origins
of those shots that seem to be coming from the direction of
Kulumani. But I'm stuck, anchored to the floor where I've just
loved as I've never loved before. Next to me, the only woman in
the universe is asleep. Half dressed, Luzilia lies in repose on the
bed, as if that dank, mildewy guesthouse were her palace.

How I missed being awake!

Luzilia stretches as if she were being born. I've been watching her for hours, in the half-light of this guesthouse in Palma.

Have you been looking at me for long?

Forever.

Well, I woke up as if I'd been sleeping forever. And you?

I heard shots a little while ago. They were coming from the direction of Kulumani. I've got to go.

Luzilia doesn't seem to have been listening. She gets dressed with that slowness that only happiness confers. Then she sits down again and hugs the pillow as she speaks.

I dreamed of a madwoman, one I knew because she was a patient at my hospital. Do you know what she did?

The woman collected butterflies; she would scrape their wings and keep the pollen in a jar. What did she do with this pollen? She filled her own pillow. Like that, she flew away while she slept.

This pillow must be packed with pollen.

I dangle the car keys in my hand. Luzilia understands the message. She suggests I go back to Kulumani and return to fetch her later. She wants to sleep a bit longer, extend her time as a butterfly in search of new wings.

Palma is a small town. If there are two vehicles, they are bound to pass each other in its streets. I almost collide with the car in which Florindo Makwala is traveling. He rolls down his window, and without getting out of the jeep, wants to know what I'm doing there, far from the village.

I've been hunting over this way. But I heard shots coming from the village.

They've killed the lions. My men have killed the lions.

So what is the administrator of Kulumani doing here? Shouldn't he be celebrating with his men, with his loyal people?

Naftalinda was injured, and I brought her to the hospital. Nothing very serious, but she's got to stay there.

Did anyone else get injured?

Genito was killed.

Genito killed the lioness, Maliqueto killed the lion. The only thing left for me to do, the last hunter in the world, is to verify the success of these shameless killers. The only thing left for me, Archangel Bullseye, who knew about bullets but not about writing, is to write up the report of the incident.

But the administrator doesn't want me to leave for the village just yet. He asks me to stop for a few minutes at the clinic. Naftalinda would be very happy to see me. Afterward, we would return together to Kulumani.

The First Lady occupies a private room. The sheets cover her vast body somewhat parsimoniously. Naftalinda's shoulder is swathed in a large bandage, which looks like a minute rag on her. The woman takes my hand and looks at me with a maternal air:

I have a request to make. Take Mariamar with you to Maputo.

Mariamar?

She's Hanifa's youngest daughter. Next week I'll be going back there too, and I'll look after her.

Don't worry, I'll take her.

You're a good man—you remind me of Raimundo, the village blind man. You have something in common, there's something uncanny . . .

Uncanny?

That man is out and about at night, he sleeps out in the open. And yet he was always spared by the lions. Do you know why he was never attacked?

Don't tell me he's one of the lion-men?

On the contrary. It's because, of all the villagers, he's the only one who is a complete person, a complete human being. Just like you, our hunter—

And now me, Makwala butts in.

Yes, you as well. You've become my man again, my dear Florindo. Then she turns to me again: *If you'd seen him last night . . .*

I've got to go, Dona Naftalinda, I excuse myself politely.

Let me look at you. You look so happy, so young.

Last night I slept in good company.

So did I. Last night I was happy, after such a long time. Even with my pains, I was well loved, I slept well and dreamed well.

Naftalinda dreamed that her mother was lulling her once again in her arms. But she sang to her in Portuguese, which in real life never happened. All the lullabies were in Shimakonde.

Until yesterday, she says, *my dreams couldn't speak with my memories. Last night they could. Last night I was lulled by time.*

On the way back, Florindo confesses that he's going to quit his post. He's going to be a teacher again. It's not out of choice, but he's resigned to it.

If it was down to me, I like politics more. But with Naftalinda, it just won't work. Then, after a pause, he adds: *You'll write up your report on the hunt, I'll write up the indictment against those who raped Tandi.*

Tell me what happened with Genito.

It was a simple but enigmatic story, like everything that happens in Kulumani. The man had succumbed while killing the lioness, next to the road. The same lioness that had attacked Naftalinda and Mariamar.

Was Genito taken by surprise?

The administrator didn't know the details. But he did know that the tracker and the lioness died together in mutual embrace, as if they both recognized each other as close relatives.

It was very difficult to pull their bodies apart. It was like a reverse birth. Apparently the writer even shed a tear. He couldn't even take a photo of them.

I imagine the writer and his tear. Certainly an invented tear, just like the word he had created. And then I think the journey was worth it for him. Gustavo Regalo now knows what a lion is. And he knows even better what a man is. He'll never again ask the reason for hunting. Because there's no answer. Hunting happens independently of reason: It's a passion, a giddy hallucination.

Are you sad you weren't the one to kill the lions? Gustavo asks, point-blank.

Me, sad?

I know what you're going to answer. That you don't kill, you hunt.

I spent the night with the woman of my dreams. How can I be sad? For sure, maybe I'll now want all the nights time has to offer. The hunter is a man addicted to miracles. The hunter is a demon saint.

Mariamar's Version

EIGHT

Blood of a Beast, a Woman's Tear

When the spiders join their webs, they can tether a lion.
—AFRICAN PROVERB

I now admit what I should have announced at the beginning: I was never born. Or rather: I was born dead. Even now, my mother is still waiting for my birth cry. Only women know how much one dies and how much one is born at the moment of delivery. For it's not that two bodies separate: It's the tearing apart of one body that was trying to preserve two lives. It's not the physical pain that most distresses the woman at that moment. It's another pain. It's part of you that is detached, the gouging of a road that gradually devours our children, one by one.

That's why there's no greater suffering than giving birth to a lifeless body. They placed that inanimate creature in my mother's arms and left the room. They say she sang me a lullaby, reciting the same mantra with which she had rejoiced in previous births. Hours later, my father took my weightless body in his arms and said:

Let's lay her to rest on the bank of the river.

It's by the water that they bury those who have no name. There they left me, so that I should always remember that I was never born. The damp soil hugged me with the same affection that my mother had devoted to me in her vanquished arms. I recall that darkened embrace and I confess that I yearn for it in the same way one does for a distant grandmother.

The following day, however, they noticed that the soil of my recent grave had been turned over. Was some subterranean beast taking care of my remains? My father armed himself with a cutlass in order to defend himself from the creature emerging from the ground. He didn't get as far as using the weapon. A tiny leg ascended from the dust and turned on itself like some tumbling spar. Then the ribs, the shoulders, and the head appeared. I was being born. The same convulsed shudder, the same helpless cry of the newly born. I was being delivered from the belly from which rocks, mountains, and rivers are born.

They say that my mother aged as much as it is possible to age in that moment. To be old is to await illnesses. In that instant, Hanifa Assulua was one great malady. My father peered at my mother's grave expression and asked:

So, am I the father of a mole?

That was when a strange light came to rest on my little face. And it was then that they saw how deep my eyes were, as deep as the river's calm waters. Those present contemplated my face and were unable to withstand the heat of my gaze. My old father, fearful, stuttered:

Her eyes, those eyes . . .

A suspicion then began to stir in all of them: I was an inhuman person. No one dared say a word. But it wasn't long before my mother realized: In my eyes there were the flashes and translucence of another, distant soul. In the solitude of her distress, she asked herself the reason why my eyes were so yellow, almost solar. Had anyone ever seen such eyes in a black person? Maybe my eyes had become so luminous because they had spent so long searching the dark subterranean depths.

Murkiness, it is said, is the domain of the dead. It's not true. Just like light, the dark only exists for the living. The dead inhabit the dusk, that fissure between day and night, where time curls in on itself.

Those who live in darkness invent lights. These lights are people, voices more ancient than time. My light always had a name: Adjiru Kapitamoro. My grandfather taught me never to fear the gloom. For within it I would discover my nocturnal soul. In truth, it was the dark that showed me what I had always been: a lioness. That's what I am: a lioness in a person's body. My shape was that of a person, but my life would be a slow process of metamorphosis: my leg becoming a paw, my nails claws, my hair a mane, my chin a jaw. The transmutation has taken all this time. It could have happened more swiftly. But I was bound to my origins. And I had a mother who sang for me alone. Lullabies endowed my childhood with shadow and forestalled the animal that lay within me.

Gradually, however, something began to change in our home. As happens with lionesses, I was left to my own devices. Little by little, Hanifa Assulua abandoned me, without any guilt, without a word of comfort. As if she had realized that I had occupied her belly and dwelled in her life purely by accident.

I return home after the fight with the lioness, my back aching and my arms gashed. I don't seek out my mother. She won't help me. I only have myself to provide solace. I follow the behavior of wild animals, and curl up in a ball like a fetus. When I'm floating between sleep and wakefulness, my grandfather Adjiru appears before me. It isn't a vision. It's him, my grandfather. He's on the veranda, seated on a mat. That was his oldest throne.

Don't you want to go inside? I ask.

It's out here on the veranda that one waits, he replies.

I try to take his hand, but he spurns it. Other hands now help him, he explains. Then he asks me to listen to him. I need to know some truths about my existence. He takes a deep breath, as if he knows he only has an instant, and then he spills it all out. These are the words of Adjiru Kapitamoro:

Maybe, my dear granddaughter, you believe you are not a person. There are visions that assail you, there are ravings that will forever follow you. But do not give credit to these voices. It was life that robbed you of your humanity: You were so treated like an animal that you thought you were one. But you're a woman, Mariamar. A woman in both body and soul. And that's not all: You, Mariamar, can be a mother. It was I who made up the story that you were barren, infertile. I invented such an untruth in order that no man in Kulumani would be interested in you. You would remain single, free to leave and put down roots far from here, free to have children with someone who would treat you like a woman. You found that man. That man has come back. I summoned him back to Kulumani myself. How did I do so? Well, how do you summon a hunter? I invented some lions, and the fame of these lions extended throughout the country. This is my secret: I'm not, as people thought, a carver of masks. I'm a maker of lions. Not because I'm a witch doctor, but because, ever since I died, I've become a god.

And that's why I know about past lies and future illusions. It won't be long, my granddaughter, before you are once again Mariamar Mpepe. Far from Kulumani, far from your past, far from your fear. Far from yourself.

I listen to Adjiru's long narration with my eyes closed, and I understand his motives. He doesn't want to forfeit my company. The only god left to me needs me more than I need him. That's why he insists that everything in my existence was as it should be. I was a human being, the daughter of human beings. I had become as I was, furtive and solitary, doubtful of my nature, because of mistreatment when I was a young child.

I open my eyes once more merely to confirm that Adjiru is no longer there. I breathe deeply and hear another voice deep within me. And this voice fills my head: There is no Adjiru, there are no invented lions, no gods putting the past to rights. The truth is quite different; it wasn't life that deformed me. I was invalidated as a woman ever since my birth. I visited the world of men merely to give them something to hunt. It was no coincidence that my legs were paralyzed. The wild creature in me demanded another posture, more prone to feline crawling, closer to the ground, nearer to the smells. Nor is it a coincidence that I'm infertile. My belly is made of another flesh; I am composed of souls that have been swapped.

Adjiru's apparition is already remote when I set out to see the dead lioness early this morning. Next to the road to Palma, on the red sandy verge, lies the lioness as if she is merely resting. It's the same one that attacked Naftalinda, the same one I fought. If it weren't for the bloodstain under her shoulder, no one would know she was dead. The policeman Maliqueto had been left to guard the trophy. To prevent witch doctors from coming to steal

the flesh. Witch doctors, hyenas, and vultures are the only creatures that eat the flesh of a lion. All the onlookers had got bored
and only Maliqueto is left to guard the remains.

Ignoring the policeman's presence, I prostrate myself in front
of the feline. I contemplate her open eyes, her tongue hanging
out, as if she were merely tired and thirsty. I take my clothes off
and, stark-naked, lie down next to the lioness, laying my head on
her still body. Who knows, maybe I could still hear her beating
heart. It's too late: All I can hear is the throb of my own chest.

Maliqueto gazes at me with a mixture of fear and puzzle-
ment. He looks down at the ground and says:

They took your father's body away just a short time ago.

My father's body?

Yes. Genito Mpepe died. The lioness killed him. Didn't you know?

I don't answer. I can't decide what I feel. Maybe I don't feel
anything at all. Or maybe his death had already occurred a long
time ago within me.

It was very strange, the policeman continues. *Your father didn't
seem to be aware of the danger. He walked towards the lioness without a
weapon, and they even say he spoke to her.*

Genito speaking to the lioness? Something about the story
sounds false to me. But I have long ceased trying to find any truth
in this world. I want to speak. A cavernous, incomprehensible
voice emerges from my throat. Maliqueto asks, alarmed:

What did you say?

I haven't said anything. When I try to repeat it more clearly,
I can confirm once more that I have lost the ability to speak. But
this time it's different: From now on, there will be no more words.
This is my last speech, my final piece of writing. And what I leave
here is written with the blood of a beast and a woman's tear: I
was the one who killed these women, one by one. I am the venge-

ful lioness. My sworn commitment will remain, without respite, without fatigue: I shall eliminate all the remaining women there are, until only men are left in this weary world, a desert of solitary males. With no women, with no children, the human race will end.

A match devoured by fire, that's how I see the future. The sky will follow humanity's example: It will wither away as barren as me. And no river will shelter on its banks the dead bodies of children. For there will be no more children born. Until the gods become women again, no one will be born under the light of the sun.

Tonight I shall leave with the lions. From this day on, the villages will quiver at my raucous lament and the owls, in fear, will turn into daytime birds.

For the people of Kulumani, this prophecy will be confirmation of my madness. That I had become like this because I had distanced myself so much from my gods, the ones that bring clouds and summon the rains. That my powers of reason escaped me because I had turned my back on tradition and my ancestors who preserve the peace of our village. But I only obey my fate: I'm going to join my other soul. And I shall never again feel the burden of guilt, as happened the first time I killed someone. At that stage, I was still too much of a person. I suffered from that human illness known as conscience. Now there is no more room for remorse. Because, when I reflect clearly on it, I never killed anyone. All those women were already dead. They didn't speak, they didn't think, they didn't love, they didn't dream. What was the point of living if they couldn't be happy?

For the same reason, years before, I killed my little sisters. I was the one who drowned the twins. Everyone thinks it was a boating accident, but it was I who sabotaged the craft and pushed

it out into the waves of the sea. It was much better that these little girls were never allowed to grow up. For they would only
ever have felt alive in pain, in blood, and in tears. Until one day
they would get down on their knees and beg their own executioners for forgiveness. Just as I begged Genito Mpepe all these
years.

It was I who led Silência to death's door on that fatal morning.
She was my sister, my friend. More than this, she was my other
self. For her, however, jealousy was always an insurmountable
obstacle. Silência always wanted to be me, to live like I lived, to
love whoever I loved. My sister always appropriated my dreams.
That's what happened with Bullseye, the hunter. I soon regretted telling her of my encounters with the visitor. For she accused
me of distorting the situation, as if that story belonged to her.
Deep down, she was tormented by jealousy. For she didn't have
enough soul in herself to invent another life. She was dead from
fear. That's why when she stopped living, she didn't die.

I'm coming to the end. Every end is a beginning, Adjiru Kapitamoro used to say. But not this end. This is the final conclusion,
the collapse of the very last skies. I only have one unaccom-
plished wish left: to go and see the ocean again. Maybe that's
why, as I feel myself falling asleep into my last human slumber,
the same dream invades me. The sea crashing onto the beach,
birds of foam fluttering through the air, and Archangel Bullseye
this time awakening from the sleep of a drowned man and taking
me far from Kulumani, to that place where mirages dwell and
journeys are born.

The Hunter's Diary

Flowers for the Living

I journeyed through extensive havens. But I only found shelter in the word.

—THE WRITER'S NOTEBOOKS

Florindo Makwala leads me to the dead lion, as if it were an excursion to my own failure. I didn't hunt any of the lions. My brother Roland can relax: This wasn't my last hunt. It wasn't even a hunt. And my mother, wherever she may be, can take pride in her prophecy: Hunting and I have gone our different ways.

On the way, we pass by to pick up Gustavo Regalo. I find him immersed in his usual papers.

Leave your work, and let's go and see the lion that's been shot.

It's not my work—I'm looking over your diary.

Is it worth the trouble?

Listen, I'm a writer, I know how to judge: Whoever writes like this doesn't need to hunt.

I feel a lump in my throat. Gustavo can't imagine the value of his reward. It was just a short note that began my story with Luzilia. It was the letters that caused my father to get down on his knees in front of his beloved wife. It was envy that I felt for Roland when he remained at home, seated like a king in the company of his books. I was always the one out on the street, or in the bush. What Gustavo now has given me is a home. Perhaps that's why I now offer him my old rifle. Gustavo declines. And I ask:

So can't we exchange? You hunt and I'll write.

You've given me what comes before the gun in hunting.

And we set off to see the lion, the trophy from such a costly war. The vehicle proceeds slowly over a short distance until it pauses near a hillock. Without saying a word, we get out of the jeep and follow a path next to the river. It's early morning, and the dew still glistens in tiny pearls on the grass and in the cobwebs. With his camera swaying on his chest, the writer follows me. The thorns brush my legs and arms. A trail of blood is my inheritance. I'm a hunter who bleeds more than his victim.

Who killed this lion? Gustavo wants to know.

It was Maliqueto, answers Florindo Makwala, who is walking in front. *Genito Mpepe was the one who killed the lioness, the one that attacked Naftalinda.*

The lioness had been killed beside the road. By this time she had been taken to the village, where she would be exhibited as proof of the hunt's successful outcome. That left the male, which looked majestic. That's why the administrator requested a photograph of the lion and not the lioness: The picture would have greater impact in the nation's news outlets.

A little farther ahead, next to a clump of bushes, lies the animal. Stretched out as only a feline can extend itself. It had lost its regal dignity. The most striking thing are the ticks sucking its snout. As soon as they sense the bitter taste of death, they let themselves drop like gray falling peas. I've come to see the lion, the king of the forest, and I'm absorbed with insignificant parasites. I picture one of these ticks growing and bursting like a grenade full of blood, staining the whole scene red.

Take a photo of me next to the trophy, the administrator insists, cutting a vain pose, one foot on the animal. It's an illusion I don't bother to dismantle: What is there is no longer a lion. It is empty plunder. It isn't anything more than a useless shell, a piece of skin stuffed with nothingness.

I am going to visit Hanifa Assulua. I won't stay for Genito's funeral. But at least I want to express my condolences. And apart from this, I have the task of taking her only surviving daughter with me.

Before entering the garden, I collect some wildflowers. I don't want to turn up empty-handed. As I kneel, picking among the grass, I am startled by Hanifa's voice:

Flowers again?

I want to explain that Genito is the beneficiary of my gesture.

But his widow walks swiftly on ahead of me, unwilling to listen. When we get to the shade of her front yard, she offers me a chair and she sits down on a mat. In silence, she allows the mourning women in black to mill around her. I have no words to say about the deceased. That's why I give her the flowers with only a word of explanation.

They're for Genito. Flowers for when there are no words.

What can we do? People live without asking to do so, and die without being given permission.

I'm sorry it ended like this.

It's not being a widow that hurts me. I've been a widow for a long time, she says in a matter-of-fact way the moment we have exchanged formal greetings.

What worries her is her daughter, Mariamar. She is ill and, in Kulumani, no one can provide her with any treatment.

I have the papers from the hospital confirming that she should be admitted. My daughter has gone mad.

I've spoken to the administrator. I'll take her with me. But are you going to stay here on your own?

I have graves to look after.

Your daughter will come and visit you.

Mariamar can't come back. Ever. She would be killed by the living and persecuted by the dead.

Hanifa goes into the house and returns a few minutes later leading a young girl by the hand.

This is my daughter.

The girl is wrapped in a *capulana*, which partially covers her face. She walks with lifeless steps, as if she were a scarecrow. In her hand she carries a notebook on whose cover one can read the words *Mariamar's Diary.* As her eyes meet mine, I feel bemused and uneasy. Suddenly those honey eyes transport me back to a past that seemed to have faded. I turn my face away, I'm a hunter, I know how to escape from traps. Those eyes contain so much light that they seem to darken the world. But it's a good darkness, the gentle languor of childhood. Mariamar's eyes are so clear that, without my knowing, they restore something to me that I lost long ago. Now I address her as if I were resuming a conversation that had been interrupted, and my voice almost fails me as I ask:

You've only got that notebook, aren't you taking a suitcase with some clothes?

She doesn't speak, her mother intervenes. *She's hasn't spoken since yesterday.*

Mariamar gesticulates, pointing at her notebook. Her mumbling reminds me of Roland, my poor brother, who had such an intimate relationship with words throughout his life, and now doesn't even have access to the most basic vocabulary. The girl with the honey eyes waves her arms, her *capulana* opens like a pair of wings, and her mother translates:

She says the only clothes she has are this notebook.

I give them some time, and withdraw so that the two of them, Hanifa and Mariamar, can say their goodbyes. But there is no leave-taking. A hand that lingers on a hand: That's the only exchange of words between mother and daughter. But the delay has a purpose that I almost fail to notice: The mother discreetly passes a kind of necklace to her daughter.

I like to give necklaces too, I say.

It's not a necklace, Hanifa corrects me. *What I'm giving Mariamar is our ancient thread of time. All the women in the family counted the months of their pregnancy on this long string.*

Mariamar is moved by this gift. A shadow passes over her eyes and she drops the notebook. As it lies half open on the ground, I read the first of its pages. These are the words: "God was once a woman…" I smile. At that moment, I'm surrounded by goddesses. From both sides of that farewell, in that rupturing of worlds, it's women who stitch together my own ruptured story. I contemplate the clouds as they advance with the ponderous, contorted step of pregnancy. It won't be long before it rains. In Palma, the woman I've been waiting for all my life awaits me.

Once in the jeep, with Mariamar sitting beside me, I utter a clumsy goodbye.

Goodbye, Hanifa.

Did you count the lions?

I've known how many there were ever since the day I arrived.

You know how many. But you don't know who they are.

You're right. That's a skill I'll never learn.

You know very well: There were three lions. There's still one left.

I look around as if surveying the landscape. It's the last time I shall see Kulumani. It's the last time I shall hear this woman. With due respect for final goodbyes, Hanifa Assulua whispers:

<u>*I am the last lioness. That's the secret only you know, Archangel*</u>
<u>*Bullseye.*</u>

Why are you telling me this, Dona Hanifa?

This is my confession. This is the thread of time I place in your hands.

Continue what Daughter Listed

A NOTE ABOUT THE AUTHOR

Mia Couto, born in Beira, Mozambique, in 1955, is one of the most prominent writers in Portuguese-speaking Africa. After studying medicine and biology in Maputo, he worked as a journalist and headed the AIM news agency. Couto has been awarded several important literary prizes, including the Vergílio Ferreira Prize and the Latin Union Award for Romance Literatures, among others, and he is a finalist for the 2015 Man Booker International Prize. He lives in Maputo, where he works as a biologist.